Strawberry Shortcake™

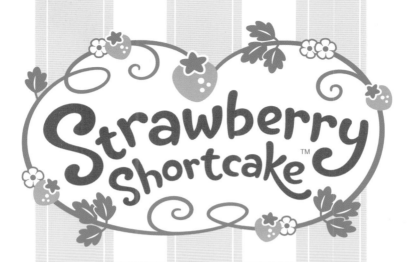

Strawberry Noir

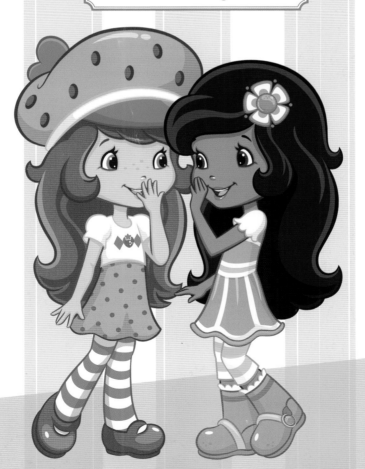

Strawberry Noir

Become our fan on Facebook **facebook.com/idwpublishing**
Follow us on Twitter **@idwpublishing**
Subscribe to us on YouTube **youtube.com/idwpublishing**
See what's new on Tumblr **tumblr.idwpublishing.com**
Check us out on Instagram **instagram.com/idwpublishing**

IDW
www.IDWPUBLISHING.com

Ted Adams, CEO & Publisher
Greg Goldstein, President & COO
Robbie Robbins, EVP/Sr. Graphic Artist
Chris Ryall, Chief Creative Officer
David Hedgecock, Editor-in-Chief
Laurie Windrow, Senior Vice President of Sales & Marketing
Matthew Ruzicka, CPA, Chief Financial Officer
Dirk Wood, VP of Marketing
Lorelei Bunjes, VP of Digital Services
Jeff Webber, VP of Licensing, Digital and Subsidiary Rights
Jerry Bennington, VP of New Product Development

ISBN: 978-1-63140-818-2   20 19 18 17   1 2 3 4

Originally published as STRAWBERRY SHORTCAKE issues #3–5.

Special thanks to Craig Herman and the entire Iconix team for their help and support.

For international rights, contact licensing@idwpublishing.com

Letters by
Tom B. Long,
Robbie Robbins, and
Christa Miesner

Series Edits by
David Hedgecock

Cover Art by
Amy Mebberson

Collection Design by
Claudia Chong

Collection Edits by
Justin Eisinger
and Alonzo Simon

Publisher
Ted Adams

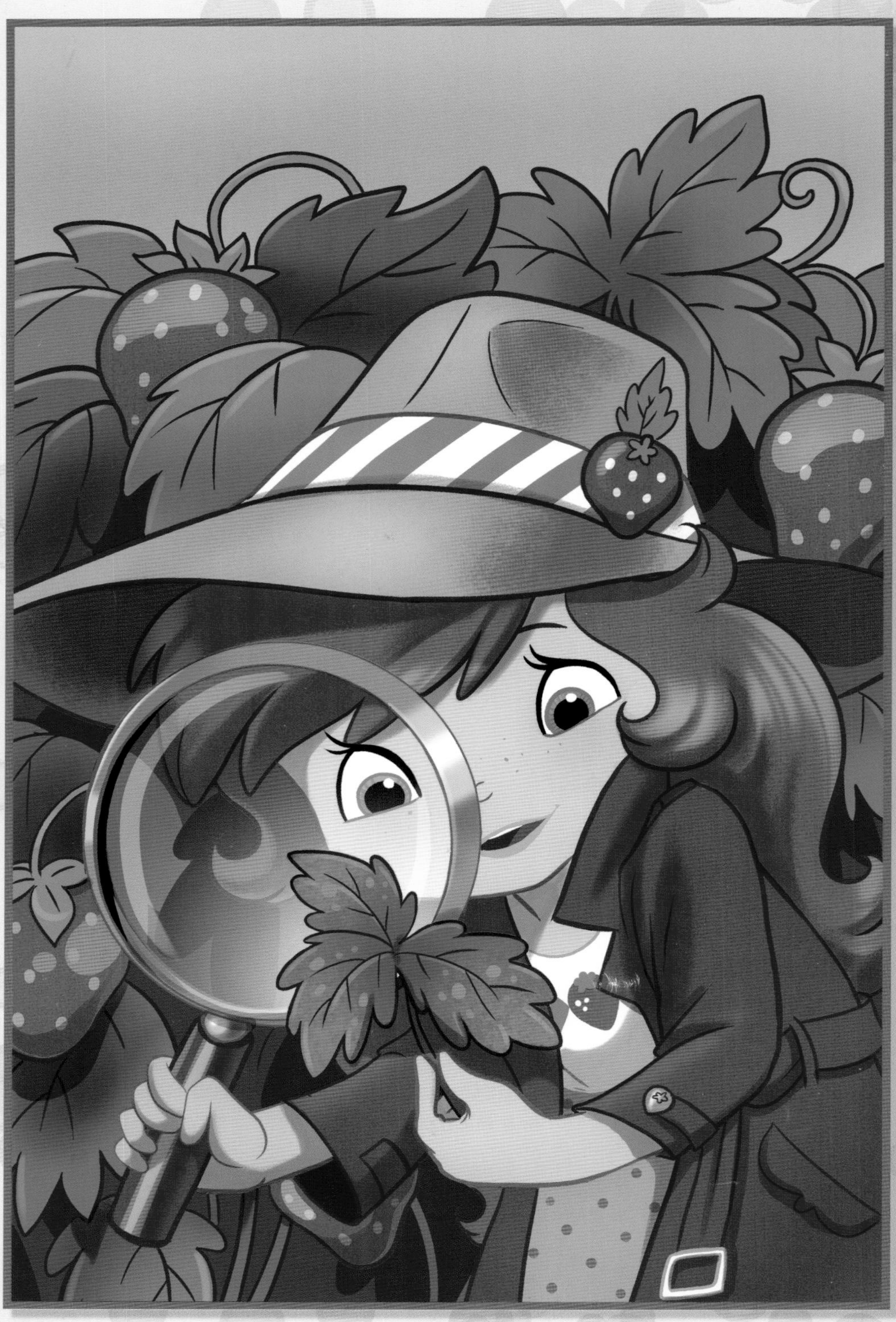

COVER ART BY
Amy Mebberson

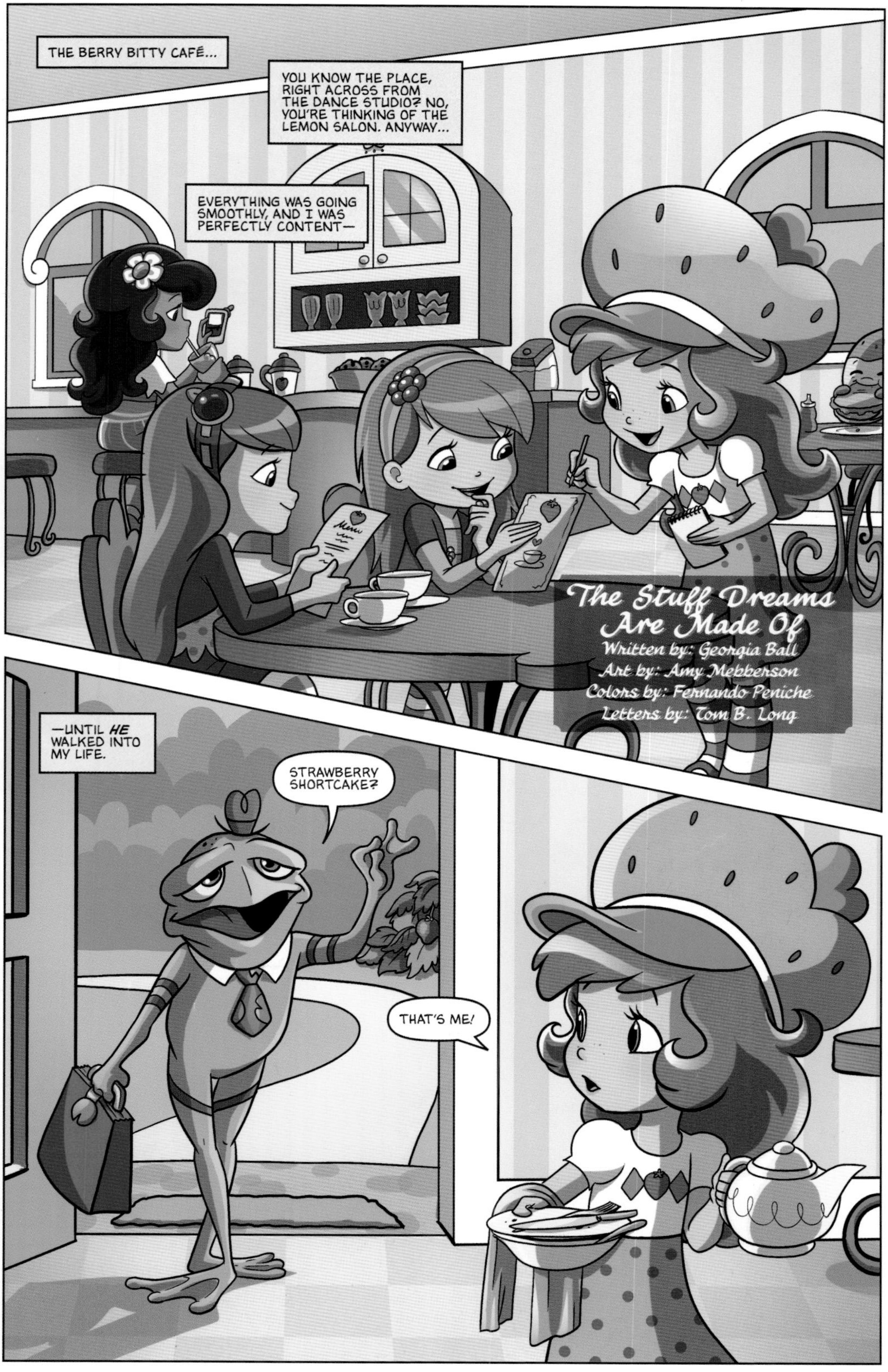
THE BERRY BITTY CAFÉ...
YOU KNOW THE PLACE, RIGHT ACROSS FROM THE DANCE STUDIO? NO, YOU'RE THINKING OF THE LEMON SALON. ANYWAY...
EVERYTHING WAS GOING SMOOTHLY, AND I WAS PERFECTLY CONTENT—
The Stuff Dreams Are Made Of
Written by: Georgia Ball
Art by: Amy Mebberson
Colors by: Fernando Peniche
Letters by: Tom B. Long
—UNTIL *HE* WALKED INTO MY LIFE.
STRAWBERRY SHORTCAKE?
THAT'S ME!

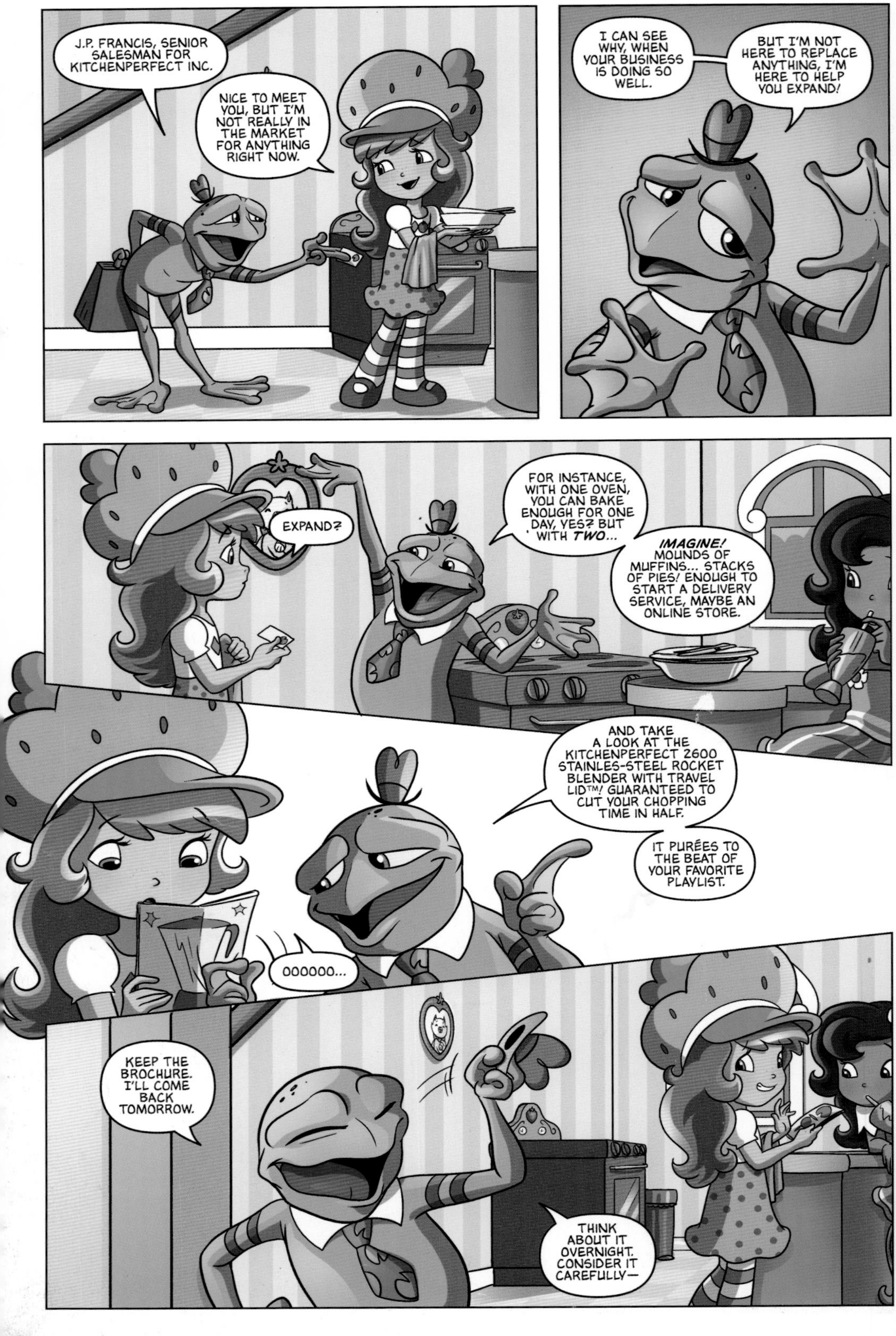
J.P. FRANCIS, SENIOR SALESMAN FOR KITCHENPERFECT INC.
NICE TO MEET YOU, BUT I'M NOT REALLY IN THE MARKET FOR ANYTHING RIGHT NOW.
I CAN SEE WHY, WHEN YOUR BUSINESS IS DOING SO WELL.
BUT I'M NOT HERE TO REPLACE ANYTHING, I'M HERE TO HELP YOU EXPAND!
EXPAND?
FOR INSTANCE, WITH ONE OVEN, YOU CAN BAKE ENOUGH FOR ONE DAY, YES? BUT WITH *TWO*...
IMAGINE! MOUNDS OF MUFFINS... STACKS OF PIES! ENOUGH TO START A DELIVERY SERVICE, MAYBE AN ONLINE STORE.
AND TAKE A LOOK AT THE KITCHENPERFECT 2600 STAINLES-STEEL ROCKET BLENDER WITH TRAVEL LID™! GUARANTEED TO CUT YOUR CHOPPING TIME IN HALF.
IT PURÉES TO THE BEAT OF YOUR FAVORITE PLAYLIST.
OOOOOO...
KEEP THE BROCHURE. I'LL COME BACK TOMORROW.
THINK ABOUT IT OVERNIGHT. CONSIDER IT CAREFULLY—

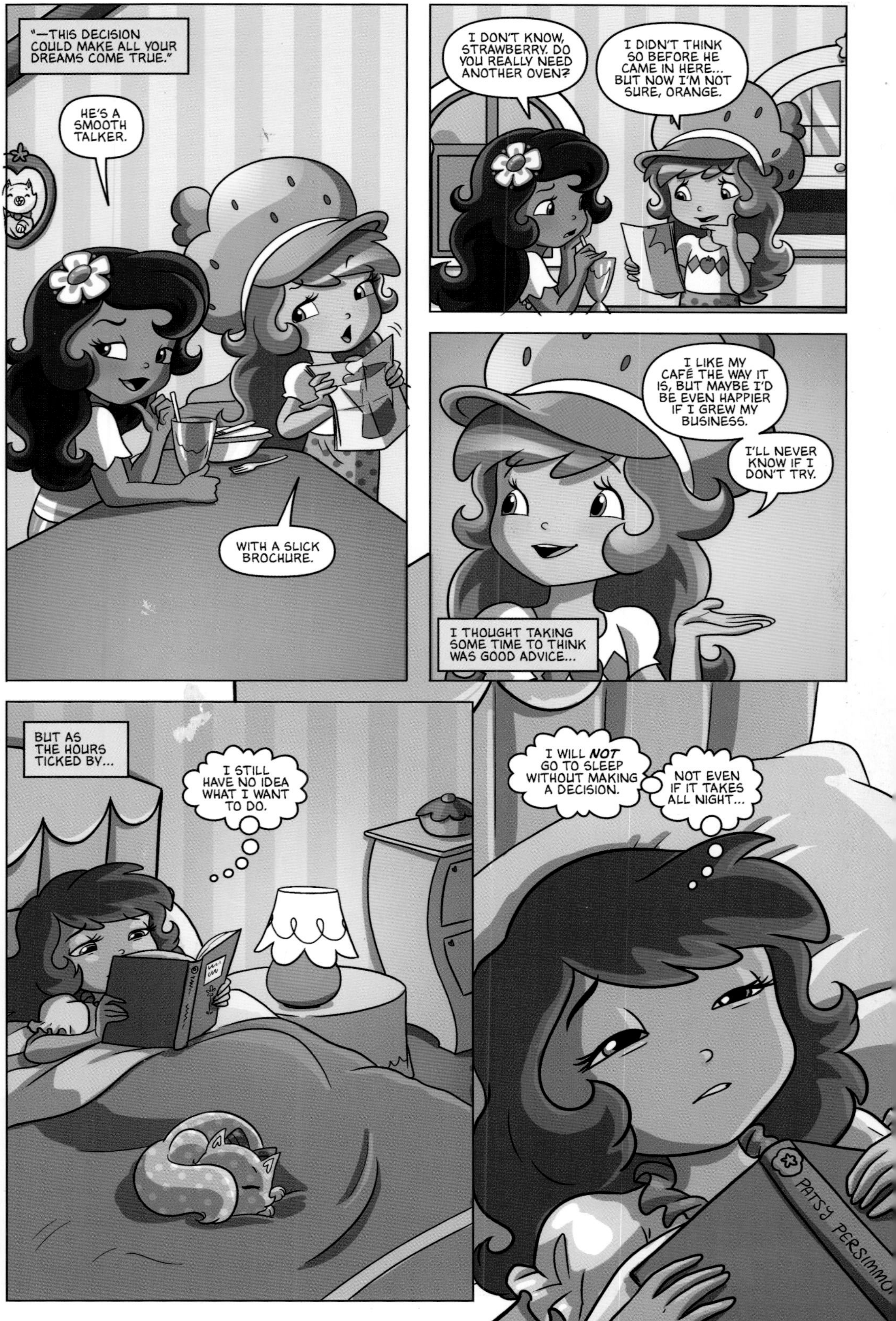
"—THIS DECISION COULD MAKE ALL YOUR DREAMS COME TRUE."
HE'S A SMOOTH TALKER.
WITH A SLICK BROCHURE.
I DON'T KNOW, STRAWBERRY. DO YOU REALLY NEED ANOTHER OVEN?
I DIDN'T THINK SO BEFORE HE CAME IN HERE... BUT NOW I'M NOT SURE, ORANGE.
I LIKE MY CAFÉ THE WAY IT IS, BUT MAYBE I'D BE EVEN HAPPIER IF I GREW MY BUSINESS.
I'LL NEVER KNOW IF I DON'T TRY.
I THOUGHT TAKING SOME TIME TO THINK WAS GOOD ADVICE...
BUT AS THE HOURS TICKED BY...
I STILL HAVE NO IDEA WHAT I WANT TO DO.
I WILL ***NOT*** GO TO SLEEP WITHOUT MAKING A DECISION.
NOT EVEN IF IT TAKES ALL NIGHT...
PATSY PERSIMMO

I NEEDED TO GIVE THIS PROBLEM MY FULL ATTENTION...

ZZZZZZZZZZZZZZZZZZ

WAKE UP, STRAWBERRY... WE HAVE A CLIENT!

SNERK

WE HAVE A WHAT-NOW?

SOMEONE HAS A CASE FOR OUR STRUGGLING DETECTIVE AGENCY?

DON'T TELL ME IT'S BEEN SO LONG YOU'VE FORGOTTEN WHAT A CLIENT LOOKS LIKE.

CASE CLOSED

I'LL GO GET HER.

A QUICK GLANCE AROUND THE OFFICE CLUED ME IN...

I'M A DETECTIVE...

LOOK AT ALL THE MYSTERIES I'VE SOLVED! LIKE THE TIME WE HELPED... THAT BEE! AND THAT TIME WE— FOUND A NEEDLE IN A HAYSTACK?

WHY WOULD ANYONE WANT TO FIND A *LITERAL* NEEDLE IN A HAYSTACK? COULDN'T THEY JUST GET A NEW ONE?

WE CAN REMINISCE LATER...

THIS IS LADY BERRY.

CASE CLOSED

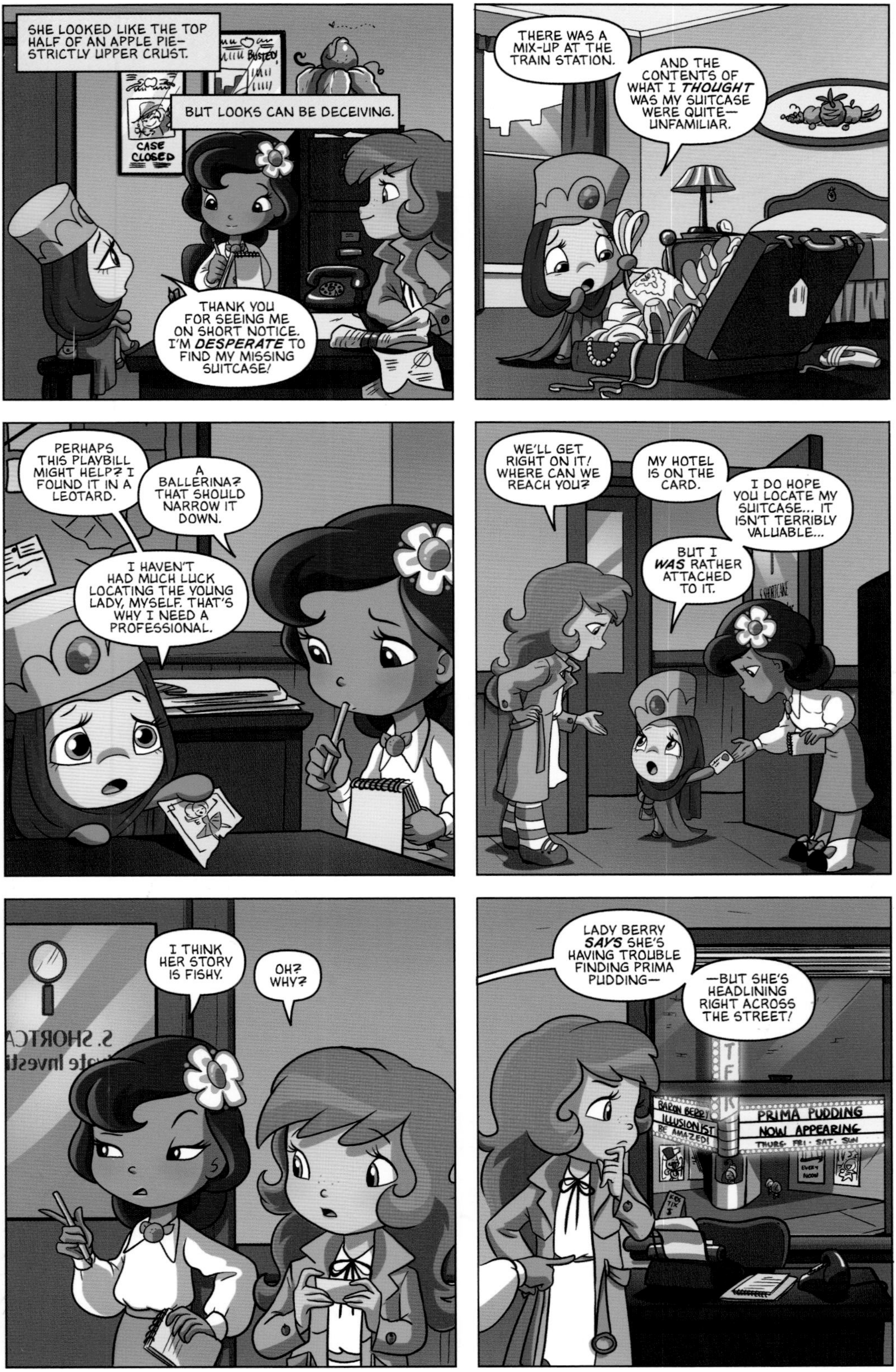
SHE LOOKED LIKE THE TOP HALF OF AN APPLE PIE– STRICTLY UPPER CRUST.
BUSTED!
CASE CLOSED
BUT LOOKS CAN BE DECEIVING.
THANK YOU FOR SEEING ME ON SHORT NOTICE. I'M *DESPERATE* TO FIND MY MISSING SUITCASE!
THERE WAS A MIX-UP AT THE TRAIN STATION.
AND THE CONTENTS OF WHAT I *THOUGHT* WAS MY SUITCASE WERE QUITE— UNFAMILIAR.
PERHAPS THIS PLAYBILL MIGHT HELP? I FOUND IT IN A LEOTARD.
A BALLERINA? THAT SHOULD NARROW IT DOWN.
I HAVEN'T HAD MUCH LUCK LOCATING THE YOUNG LADY, MYSELF. THAT'S WHY I NEED A PROFESSIONAL.
WE'LL GET RIGHT ON IT! WHERE CAN WE REACH YOU?
MY HOTEL IS ON THE CARD.
I DO HOPE YOU LOCATE MY SUITCASE... IT ISN'T TERRIBLY VALUABLE...
BUT I *WAS* RATHER ATTACHED TO IT.
I THINK HER STORY IS FISHY.
OH? WHY?
LADY BERRY *SAYS* SHE'S HAVING TROUBLE FINDING PRIMA PUDDING—
—BUT SHE'S HEADLINING RIGHT ACROSS THE STREET!
BARON BERRY
ILLUSIONIST
BE AMAZED!
PRIMA PUDDING
NOW APPEARING
THURS. FRI. SAT. SUN

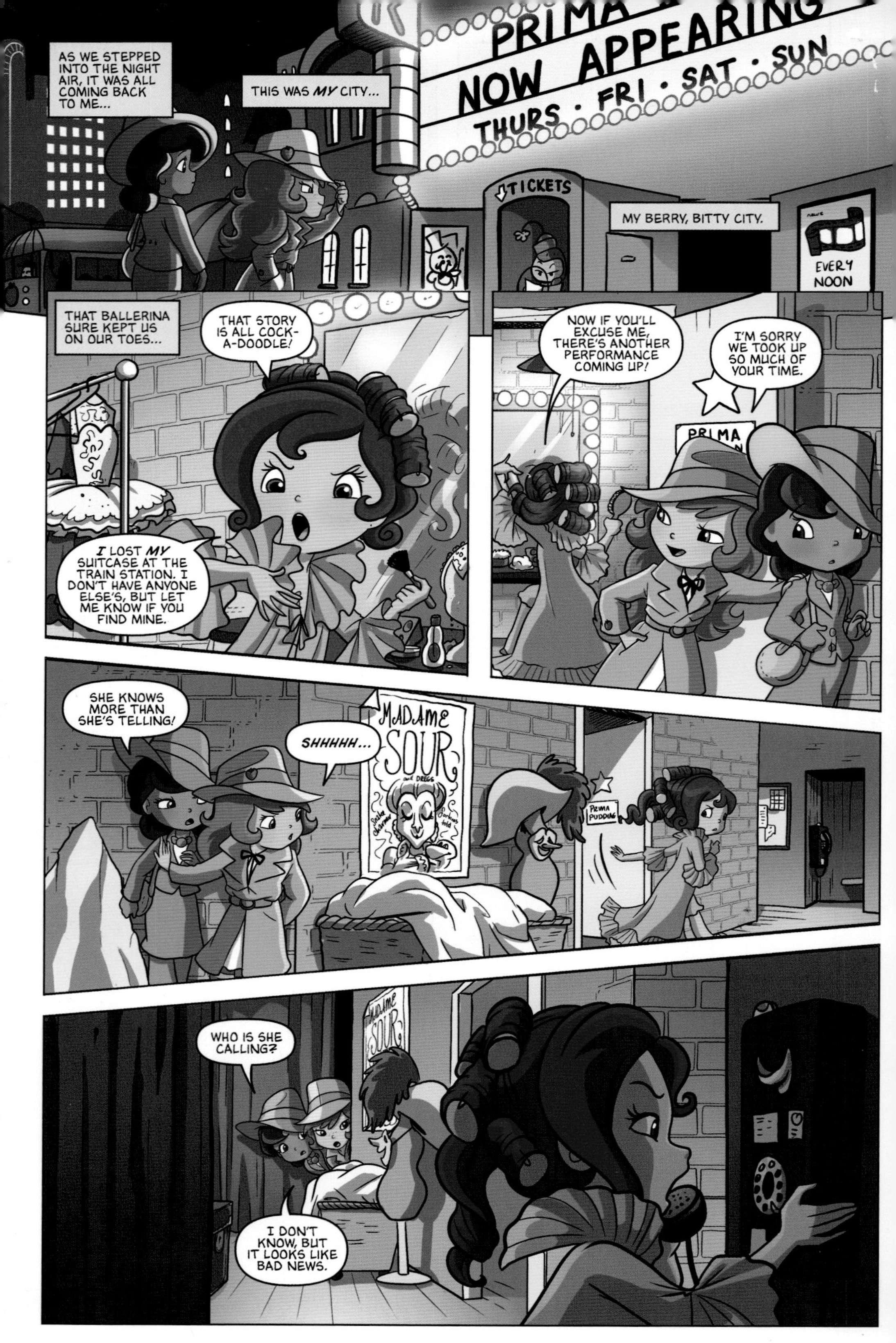
AS WE STEPPED INTO THE NIGHT AIR, IT WAS ALL COMING BACK TO ME...
THIS WAS MY CITY...
PRIMA
NOW APPEARING
THURS · FRI · SAT · SUN
TICKETS
MY BERRY, BITTY CITY.
EVERY NOON
THAT BALLERINA SURE KEPT US ON OUR TOES...
THAT STORY IS ALL COCK-A-DOODLE!
I LOST MY SUITCASE AT THE TRAIN STATION. I DON'T HAVE ANYONE ELSE'S, BUT LET ME KNOW IF YOU FIND MINE.
NOW IF YOU'LL EXCUSE ME, THERE'S ANOTHER PERFORMANCE COMING UP!
I'M SORRY WE TOOK UP SO MUCH OF YOUR TIME.
PRIMA
SHE KNOWS MORE THAN SHE'S TELLING!
SHHHHH...
MADAME SOUR
and DREGS
PRIMA PUDDING
WHO IS SHE CALLING?
MADAME SOUR
I DON'T KNOW, BUT IT LOOKS LIKE BAD NEWS.

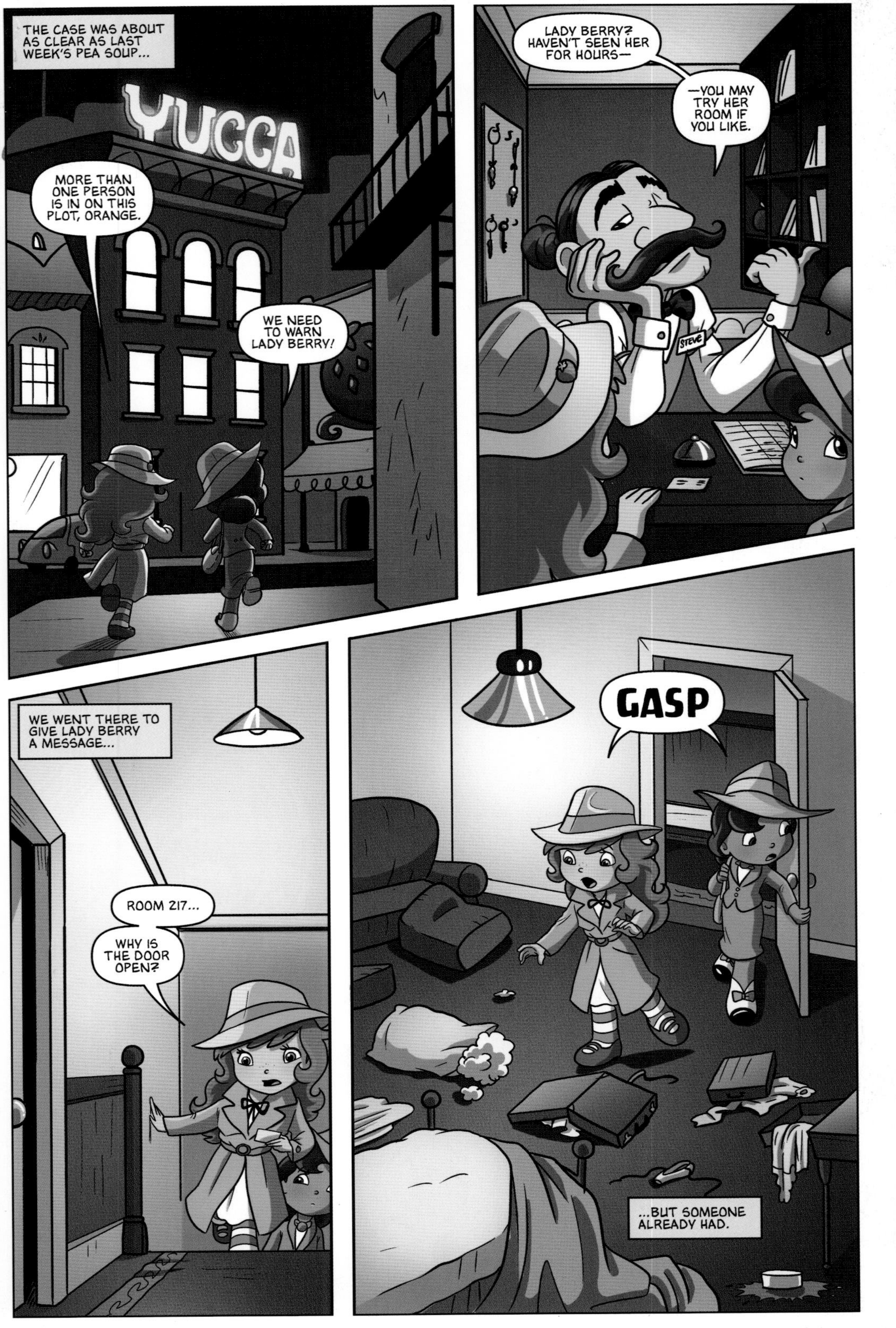
THE CASE WAS ABOUT AS CLEAR AS LAST WEEK'S PEA SOUP...
YUCCA
MORE THAN ONE PERSON IS IN ON THIS PLOT, ORANGE.
WE NEED TO WARN LADY BERRY!
LADY BERRY? HAVEN'T SEEN HER FOR HOURS—
—YOU MAY TRY HER ROOM IF YOU LIKE.
STEVE
WE WENT THERE TO GIVE LADY BERRY A MESSAGE...
ROOM 217...
WHY IS THE DOOR OPEN?
GASP
...BUT SOMEONE ALREADY HAD.

THE SOUP THICKENS!

WHAT IF SHE'S BEEN KIDNAPPED?

THEN WE HAVE A CASE WITHOUT A CLIENT!

. SHORTCAKE
vate Inve

MAYBE SHE'S JUST A REALLY MESSY GUEST...

WHAT?

WHOOSH

THIS ISN'T WHAT IT LOOKS LIKE, I ASSURE YOU.

THAT'S GOOD BECAUSE IT TOTALLY LOOKED LIKE YOU WERE SEARCHING MY DESK.

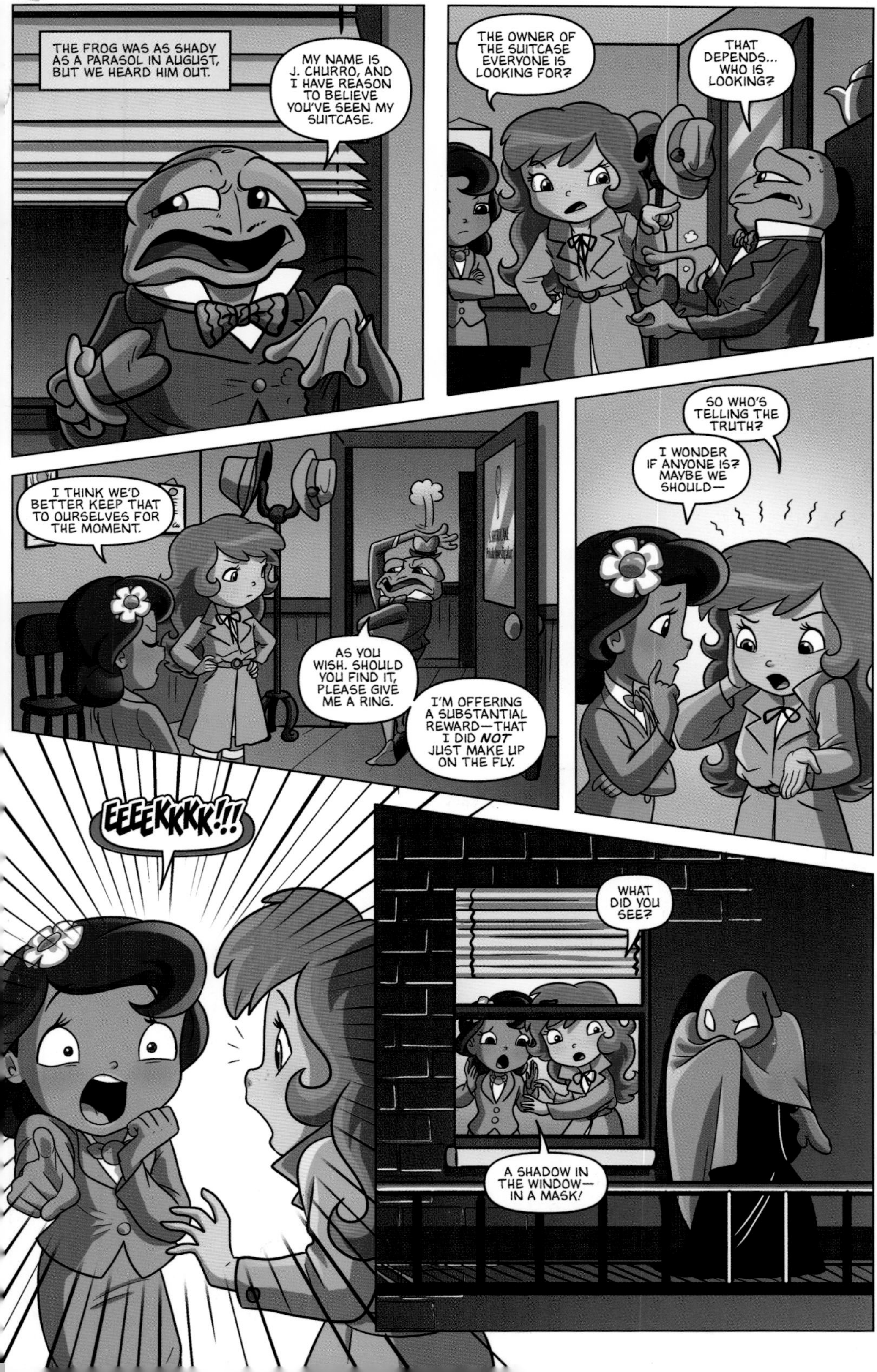
THE FROG WAS AS SHADY AS A PARASOL IN AUGUST, BUT WE HEARD HIM OUT.
MY NAME IS J. CHURRO, AND I HAVE REASON TO BELIEVE YOU'VE SEEN MY SUITCASE.
THE OWNER OF THE SUITCASE EVERYONE IS LOOKING FOR?
THAT DEPENDS... WHO IS LOOKING?
I THINK WE'D BETTER KEEP THAT TO OURSELVES FOR THE MOMENT.
AS YOU WISH. SHOULD YOU FIND IT, PLEASE GIVE ME A RING.
I'M OFFERING A SUBSTANTIAL REWARD—THAT I DID *NOT* JUST MAKE UP ON THE FLY.
SO WHO'S TELLING THE TRUTH?
I WONDER IF ANYONE IS? MAYBE WE SHOULD—
EEEEKKKK!!!
WHAT DID YOU SEE?
A SHADOW IN THE WINDOW— IN A MASK!

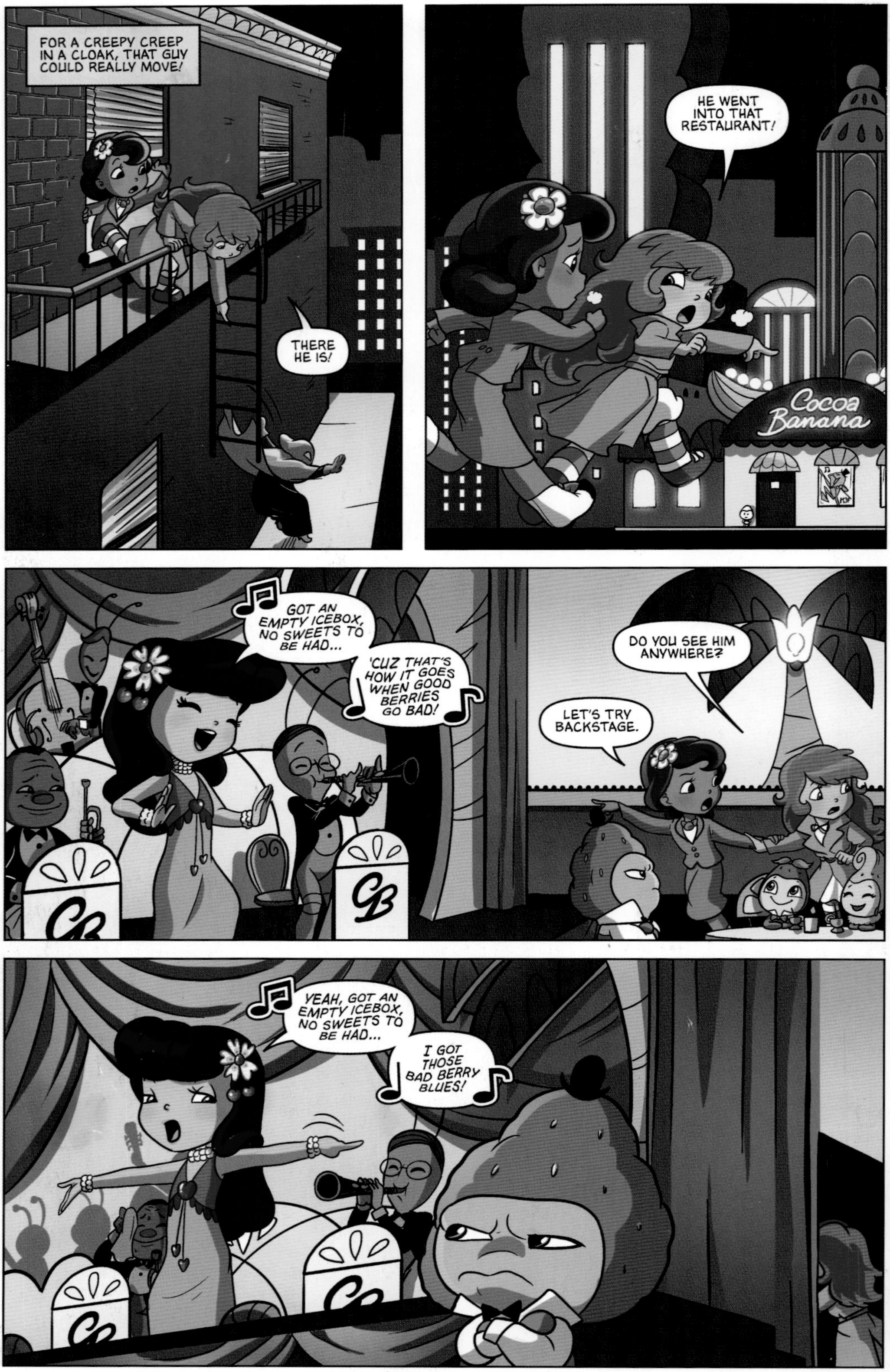
FOR A CREEPY CREEP IN A CLOAK, THAT GUY COULD REALLY MOVE!
THERE HE IS!
HE WENT INTO THAT RESTAURANT!
Cocoa Banana
GOT AN EMPTY ICEBOX, NO SWEETS TO BE HAD...
'CUZ THAT'S HOW IT GOES WHEN GOOD BERRIES GO BAD!
DO YOU SEE HIM ANYWHERE?
LET'S TRY BACKSTAGE.
YEAH, GOT AN EMPTY ICEBOX, NO SWEETS TO BE HAD...
I GOT THOSE BAD BERRY BLUES!

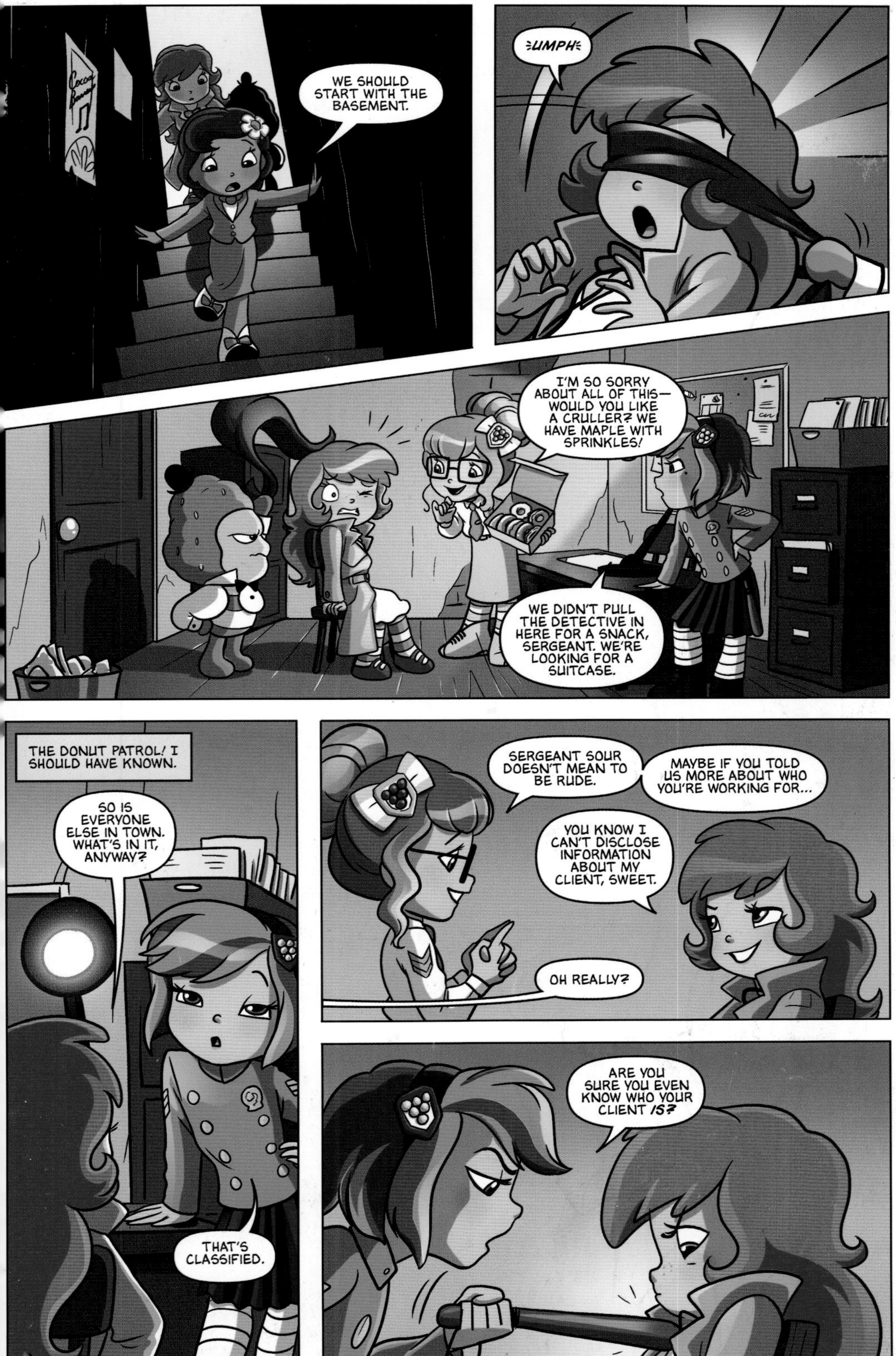
WE SHOULD START WITH THE BASEMENT.
UMPH
I'M SO SORRY ABOUT ALL OF THIS— WOULD YOU LIKE A CRULLER? WE HAVE MAPLE WITH SPRINKLES!
WE DIDN'T PULL THE DETECTIVE IN HERE FOR A SNACK, SERGEANT. WE'RE LOOKING FOR A SUITCASE.
THE DONUT PATROL! I SHOULD HAVE KNOWN.
SO IS EVERYONE ELSE IN TOWN. WHAT'S IN IT, ANYWAY?
THAT'S CLASSIFIED.
SERGEANT SOUR DOESN'T MEAN TO BE RUDE.
MAYBE IF YOU TOLD US MORE ABOUT WHO YOU'RE WORKING FOR...
YOU KNOW I CAN'T DISCLOSE INFORMATION ABOUT MY CLIENT, SWEET.
OH REALLY?
ARE YOU SURE YOU EVEN KNOW WHO YOUR CLIENT *IS*?

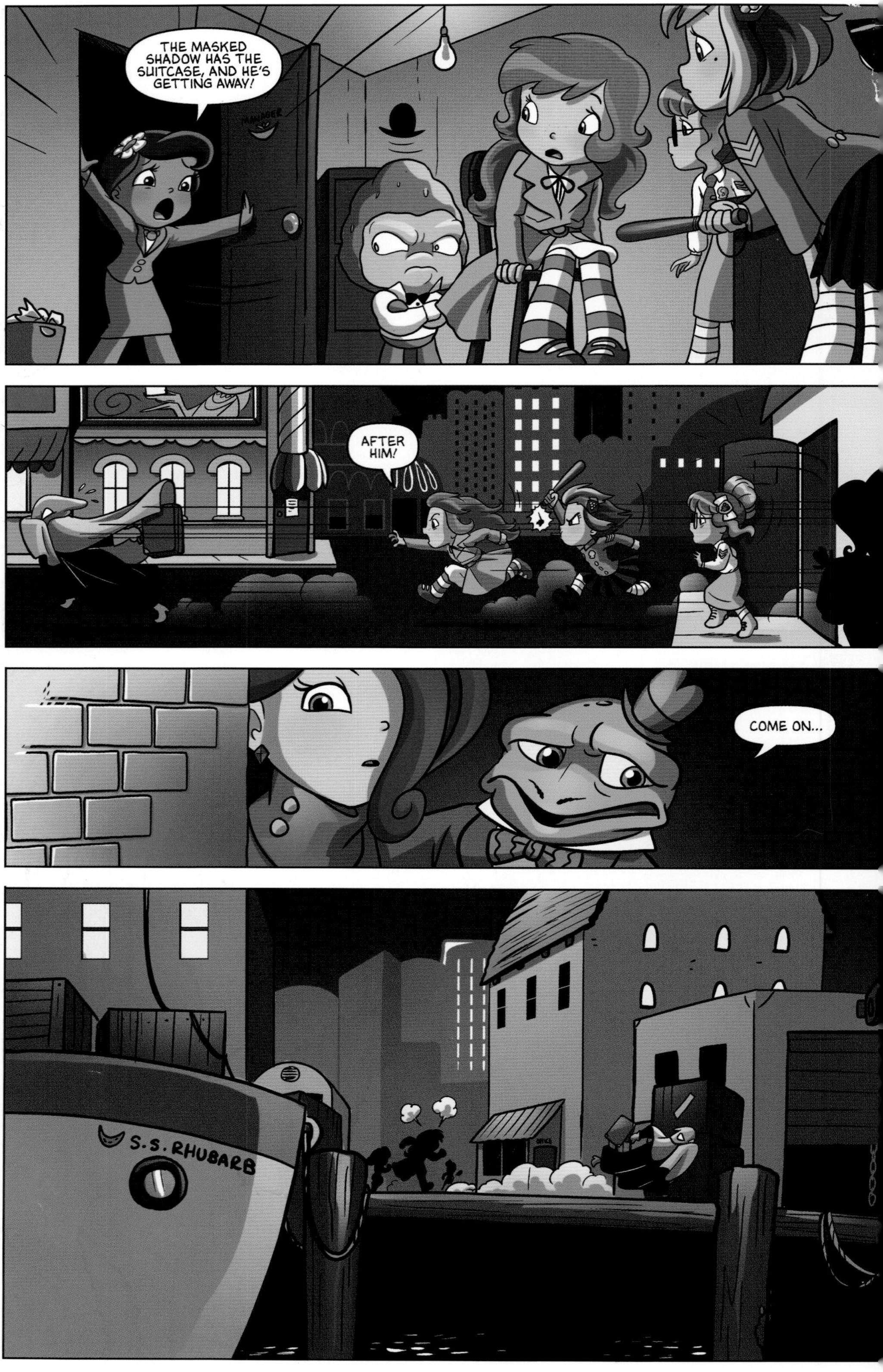
THE MASKED SHADOW HAS THE SUITCASE, AND HE'S GETTING AWAY!
MANAGER
AFTER HIM!
COME ON...
S.S. RHUBARB
OFFICE

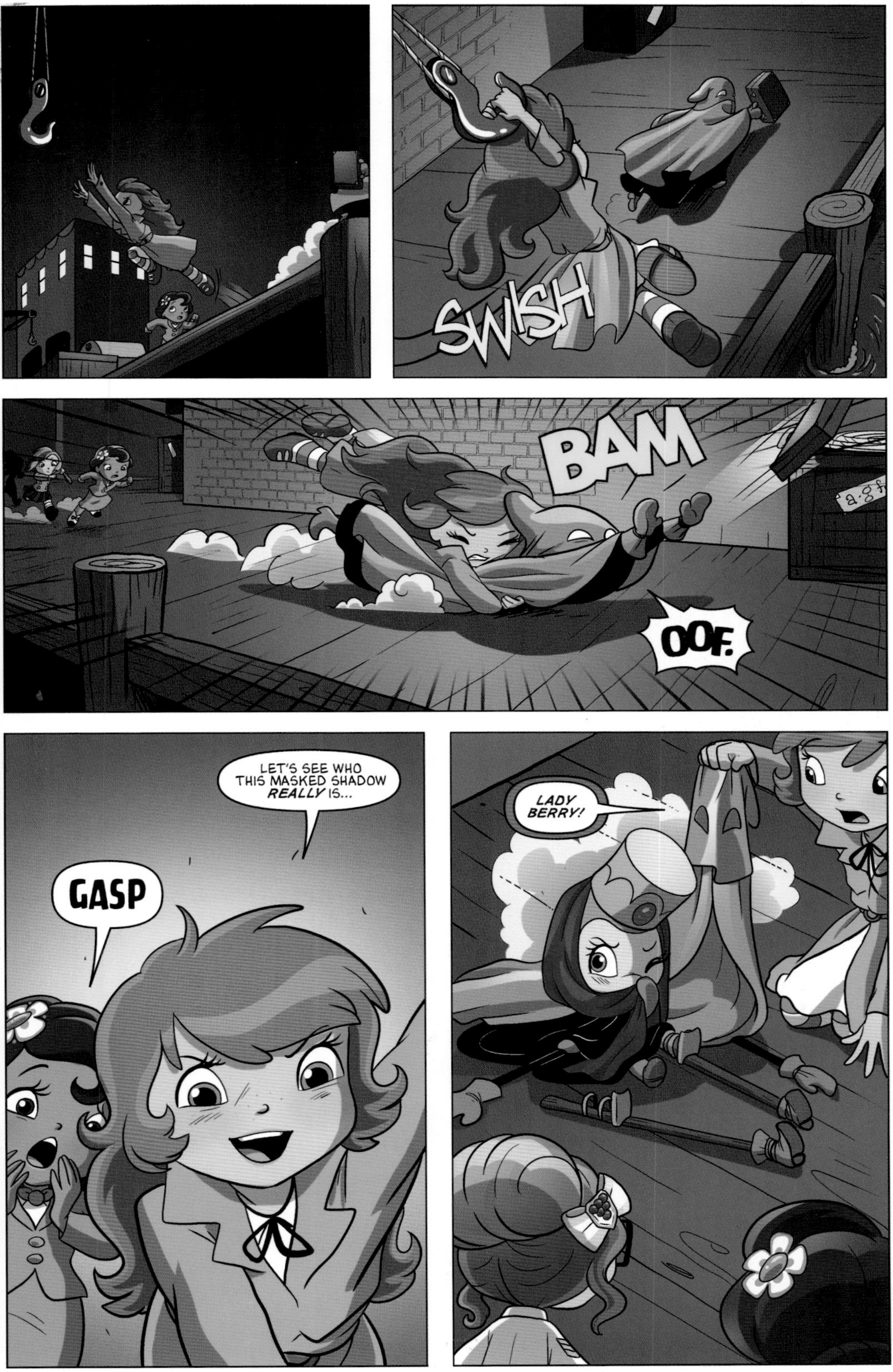
SWISH
BAM
OOF.
LET'S SEE WHO THIS MASKED SHADOW REALLY IS...
GASP
LADY BERRY!

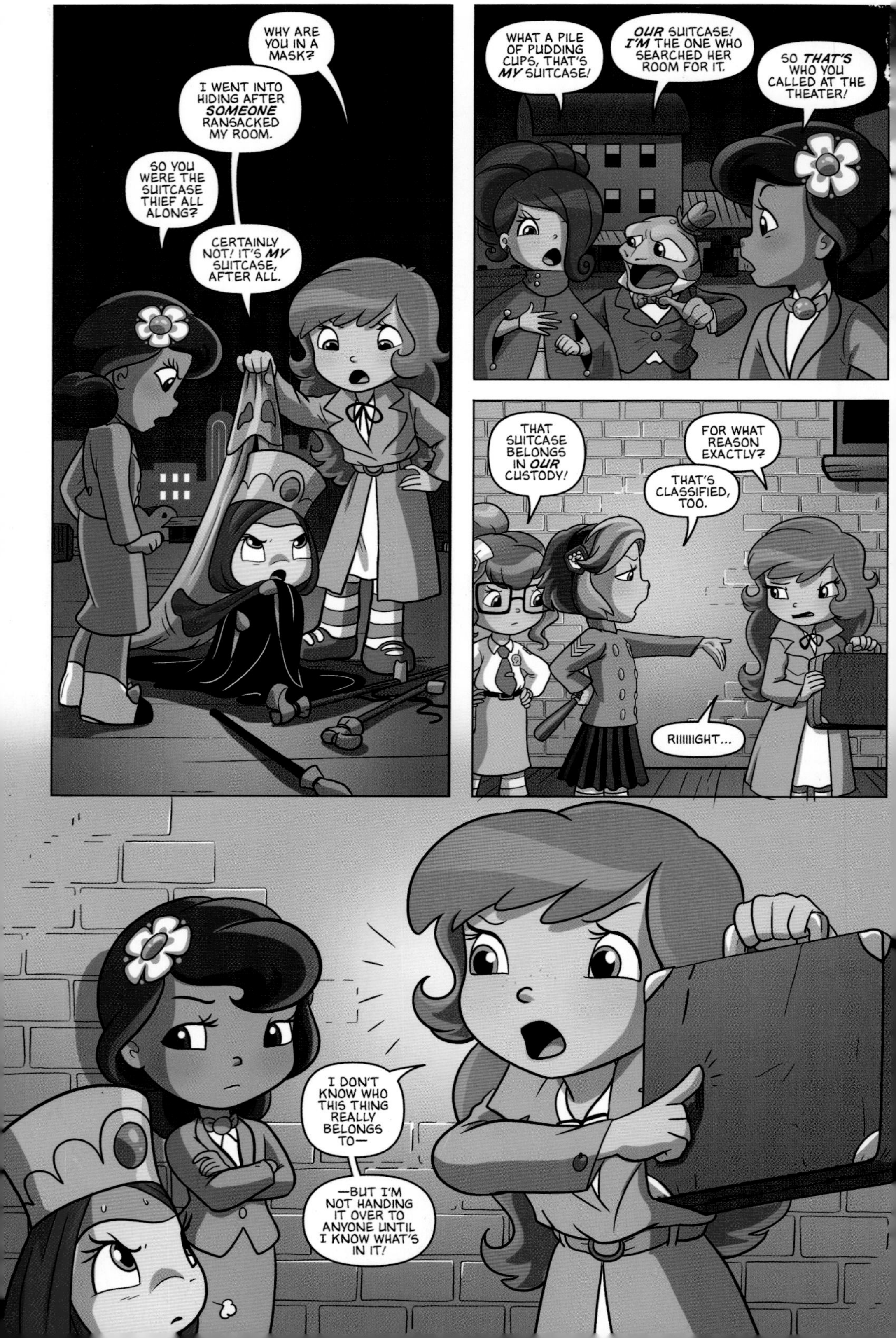
WHY ARE YOU IN A MASK?
I WENT INTO HIDING AFTER SOMEONE RANSACKED MY ROOM.
SO YOU WERE THE SUITCASE THIEF ALL ALONG?
CERTAINLY NOT! IT'S MY SUITCASE, AFTER ALL.
WHAT A PILE OF PUDDING CUPS, THAT'S MY SUITCASE!
OUR SUITCASE! I'M THE ONE WHO SEARCHED HER ROOM FOR IT.
SO THAT'S WHO YOU CALLED AT THE THEATER!
THAT SUITCASE BELONGS IN OUR CUSTODY!
FOR WHAT REASON EXACTLY?
THAT'S CLASSIFIED, TOO.
RIIIIIGHT...
I DON'T KNOW WHO THIS THING REALLY BELONGS TO—
—BUT I'M NOT HANDING IT OVER TO ANYONE UNTIL I KNOW WHAT'S IN IT!

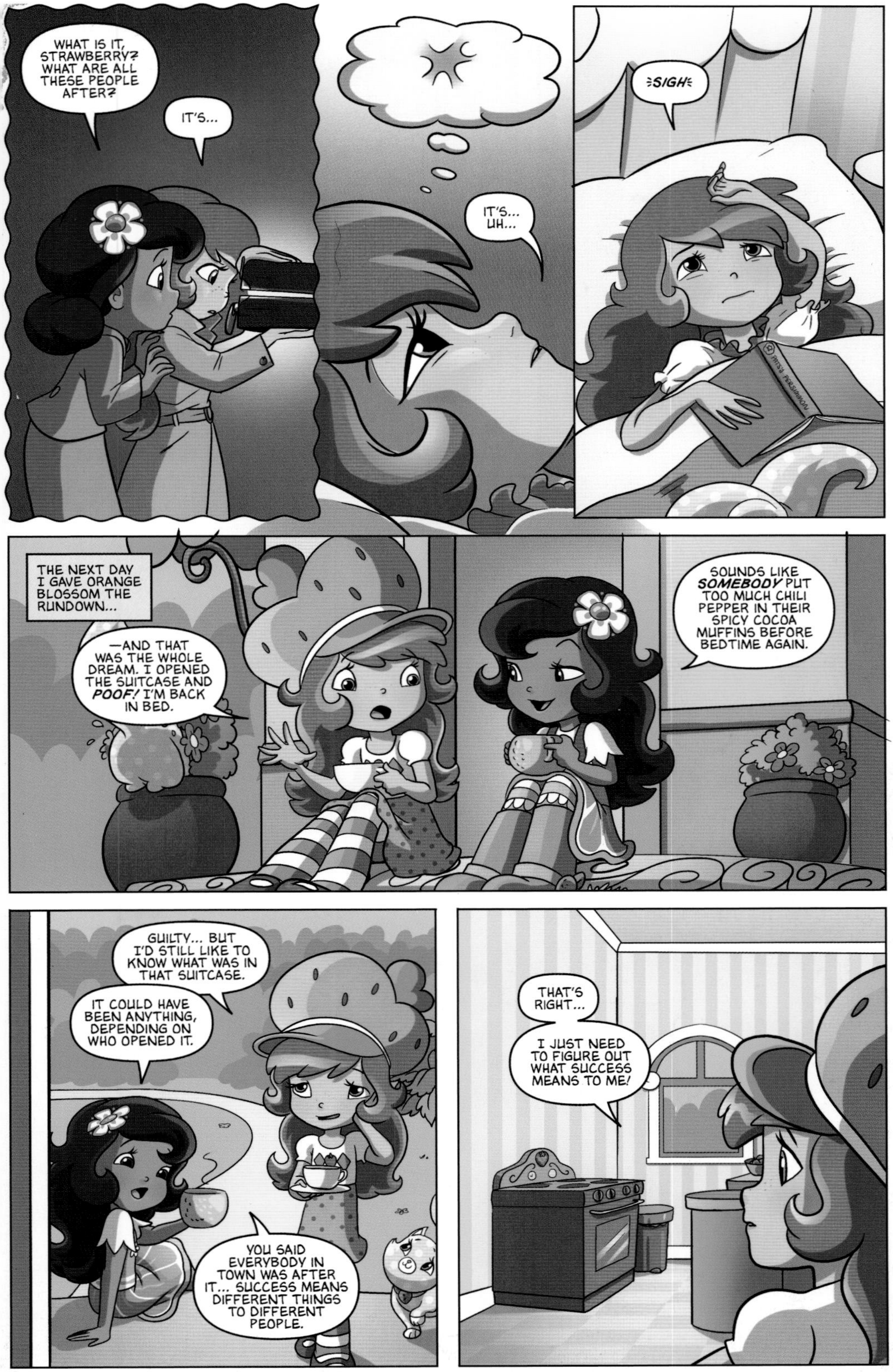
WHAT IS IT, STRAWBERRY? WHAT ARE ALL THESE PEOPLE AFTER?
IT'S...
IT'S... UH...
SIGH
THE NEXT DAY I GAVE ORANGE BLOSSOM THE RUNDOWN...
—AND THAT WAS THE WHOLE DREAM. I OPENED THE SUITCASE AND POOF! I'M BACK IN BED.
SOUNDS LIKE SOMEBODY PUT TOO MUCH CHILI PEPPER IN THEIR SPICY COCOA MUFFINS BEFORE BEDTIME AGAIN.
GUILTY... BUT I'D STILL LIKE TO KNOW WHAT WAS IN THAT SUITCASE.
IT COULD HAVE BEEN ANYTHING, DEPENDING ON WHO OPENED IT.
YOU SAID EVERYBODY IN TOWN WAS AFTER IT... SUCCESS MEANS DIFFERENT THINGS TO DIFFERENT PEOPLE.
THAT'S RIGHT...
I JUST NEED TO FIGURE OUT WHAT SUCCESS MEANS TO ME!

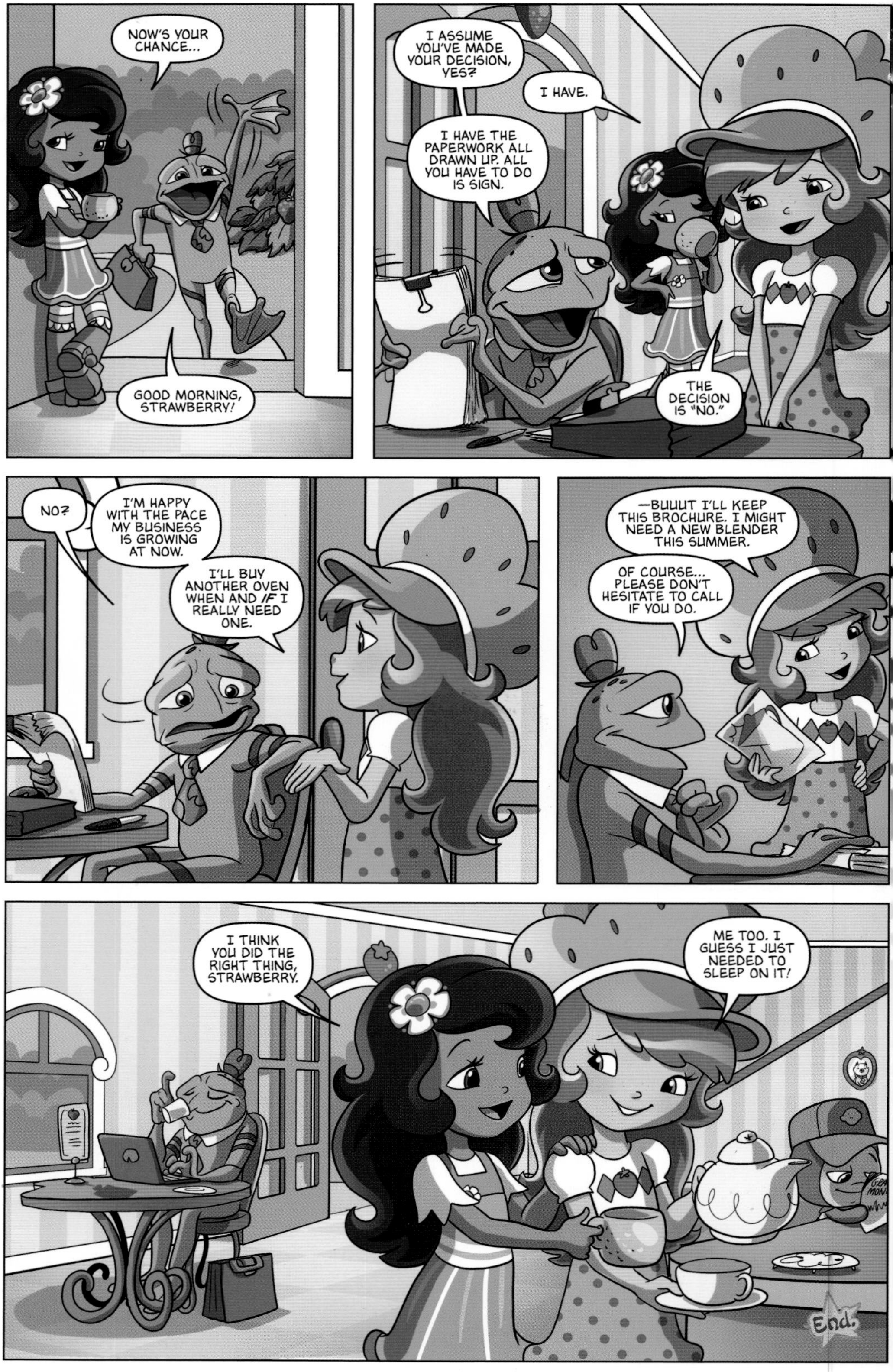
NOW'S YOUR CHANCE...
GOOD MORNING, STRAWBERRY!
I ASSUME YOU'VE MADE YOUR DECISION, YES?
I HAVE.
I HAVE THE PAPERWORK ALL DRAWN UP. ALL YOU HAVE TO DO IS SIGN.
THE DECISION IS "NO."
NO?
I'M HAPPY WITH THE PACE MY BUSINESS IS GROWING AT NOW.
I'LL BUY ANOTHER OVEN WHEN AND *IF* I REALLY NEED ONE.
—BUUUT I'LL KEEP THIS BROCHURE. I MIGHT NEED A NEW BLENDER THIS SUMMER.
OF COURSE... PLEASE DON'T HESITATE TO CALL IF YOU DO.
I THINK YOU DID THE RIGHT THING, STRAWBERRY.
ME TOO. I GUESS I JUST NEEDED TO SLEEP ON IT!
End.

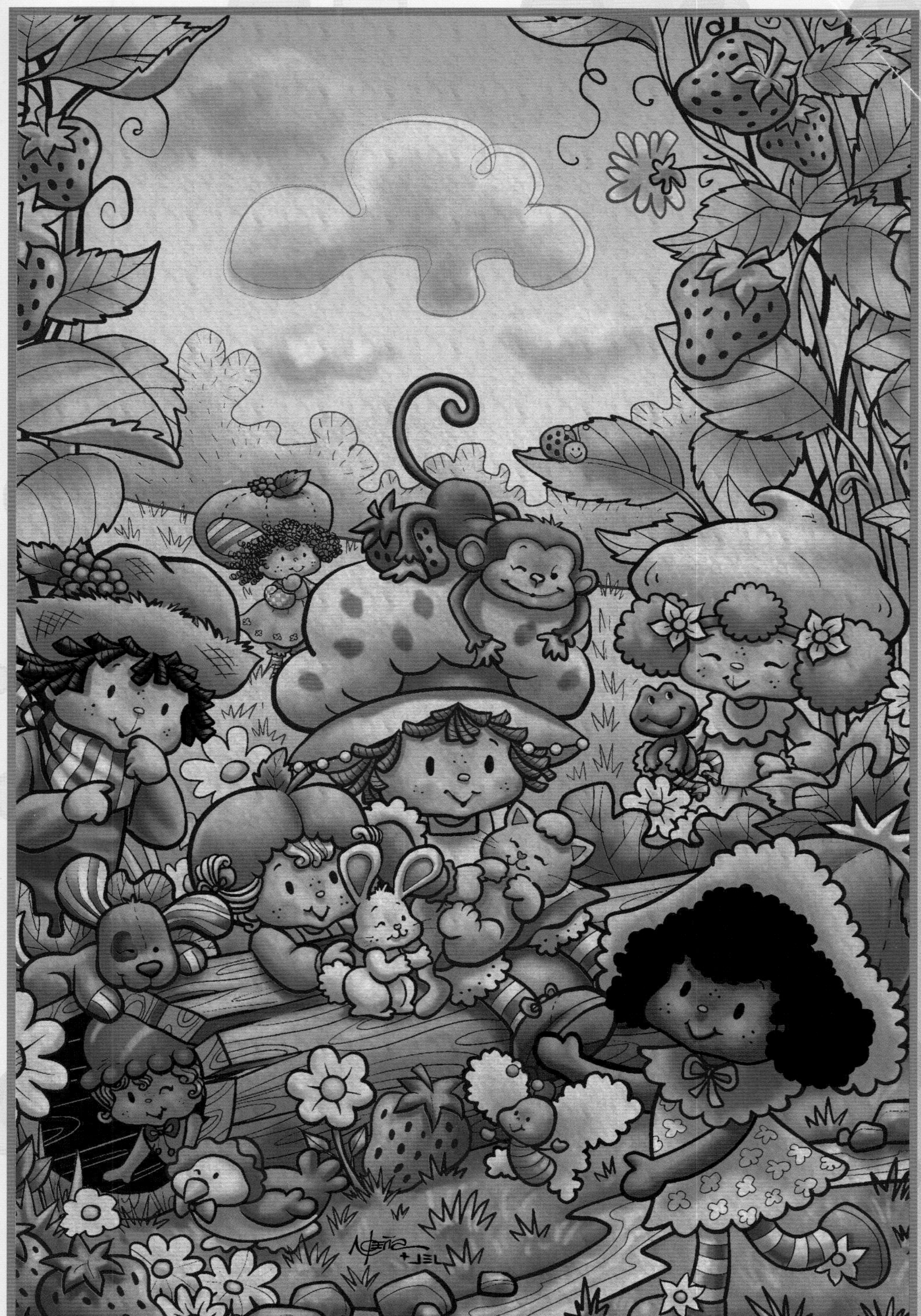

COVER ART BY **Nico Peña**
COVER COLORS BY **Jordi Escuin**

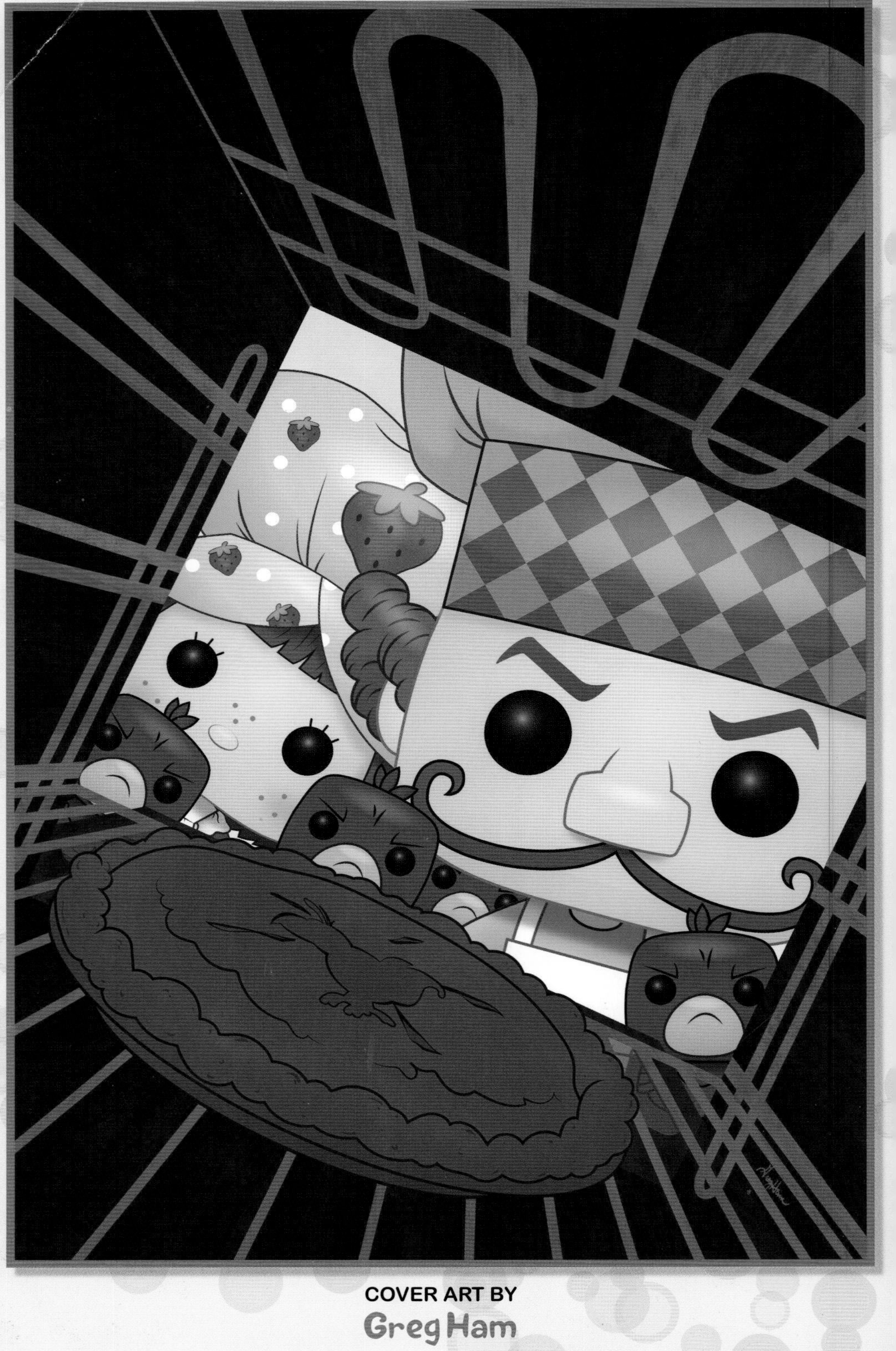

COVER ART BY
Greg Ham

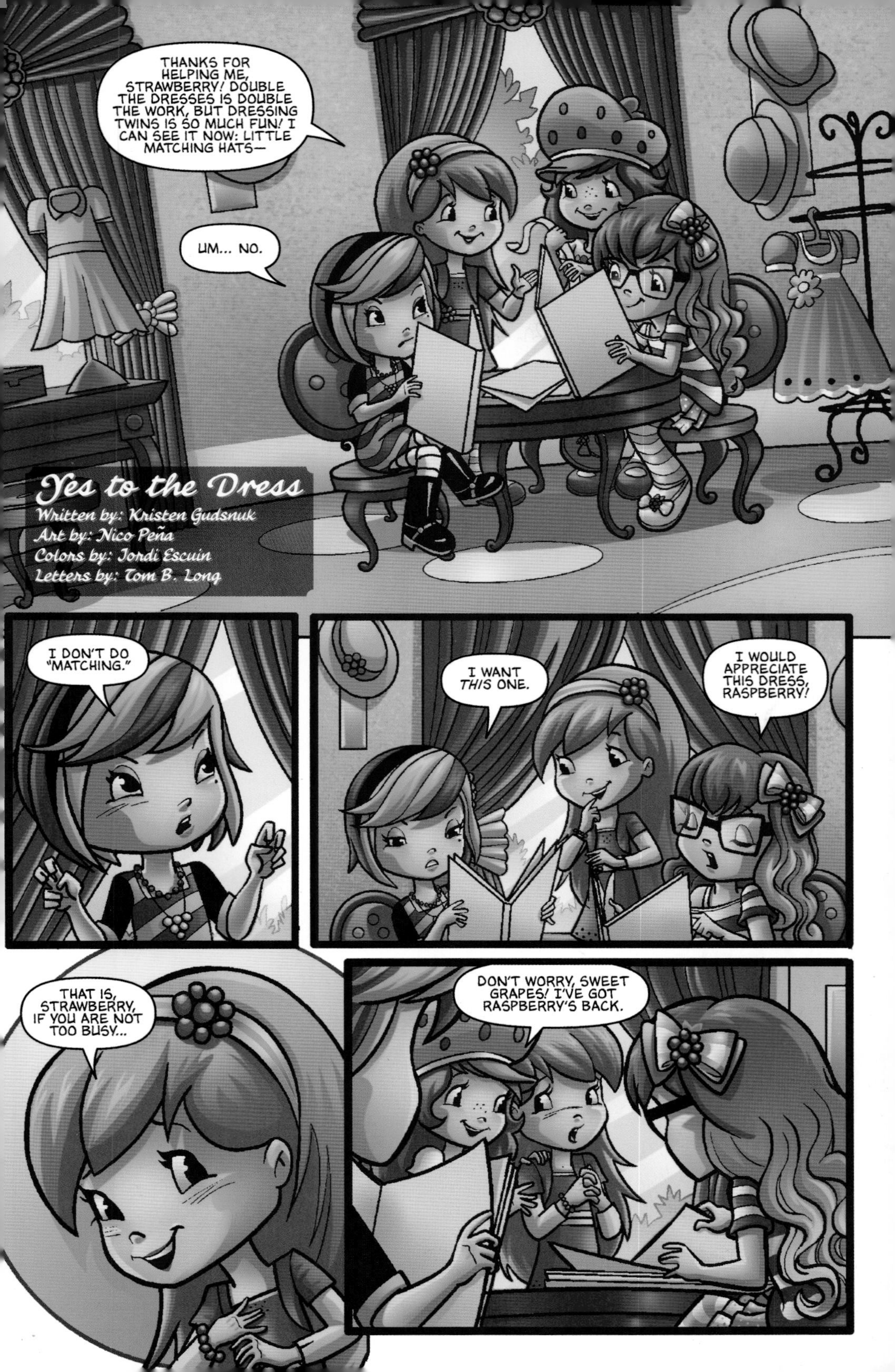
THANKS FOR HELPING ME, STRAWBERRY! DOUBLE THE DRESSES IS DOUBLE THE WORK, BUT DRESSING TWINS IS SO MUCH FUN! I CAN SEE IT NOW: LITTLE MATCHING HATS—
UM... NO.
Yes to the Dress
Written by: Kristen Gudsnuk
Art by: Nico Peña
Colors by: Jordi Escuin
Letters by: Tom B. Long
I DON'T DO "MATCHING."
I WANT *THIS* ONE.
I WOULD APPRECIATE THIS DRESS, RASPBERRY!
THAT IS, STRAWBERRY, IF YOU ARE NOT TOO BUSY...
DON'T WORRY, SWEET GRAPES! I'VE GOT RASPBERRY'S BACK.

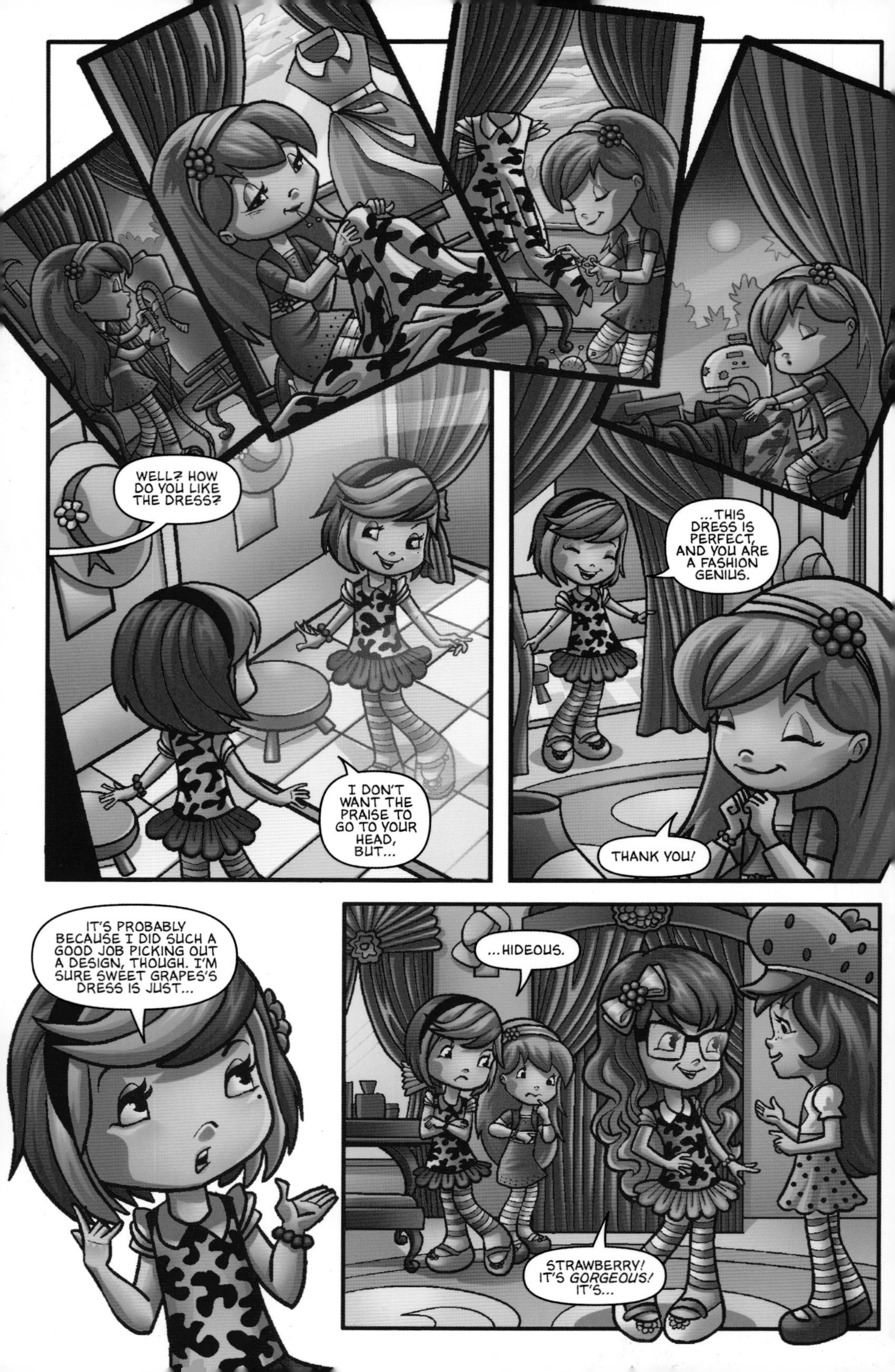
WELL? HOW DO YOU LIKE THE DRESS?
I DON'T WANT THE PRAISE TO GO TO YOUR HEAD, BUT...
...THIS DRESS IS PERFECT, AND YOU ARE A FASHION GENIUS.
THANK YOU!
IT'S PROBABLY BECAUSE I DID SUCH A GOOD JOB PICKING OUT A DESIGN, THOUGH. I'M SURE SWEET GRAPES'S DRESS IS JUST...
...HIDEOUS.
STRAWBERRY! IT'S *GORGEOUS*! IT'S...

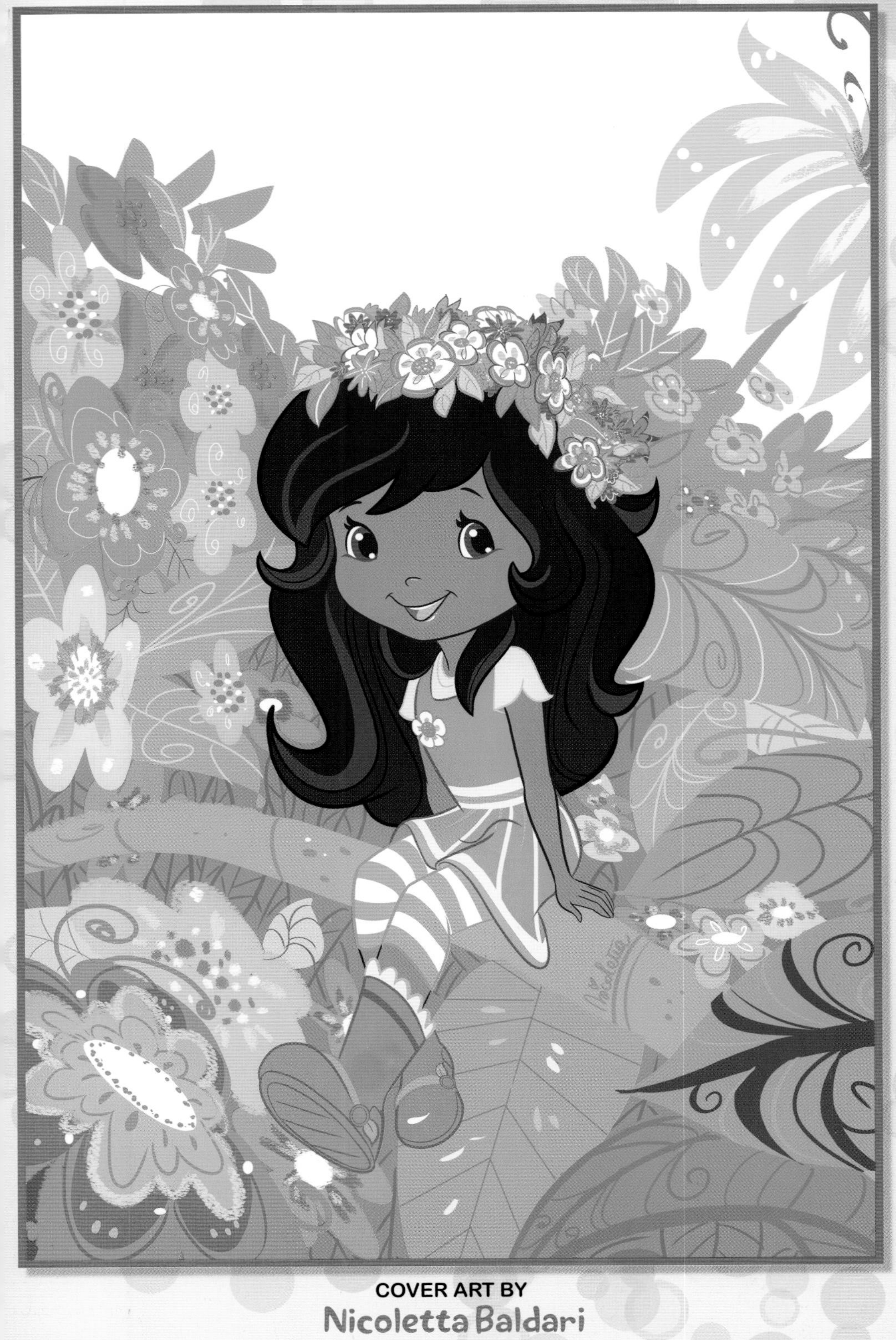

COVER ART BY
Nicoletta Baldari

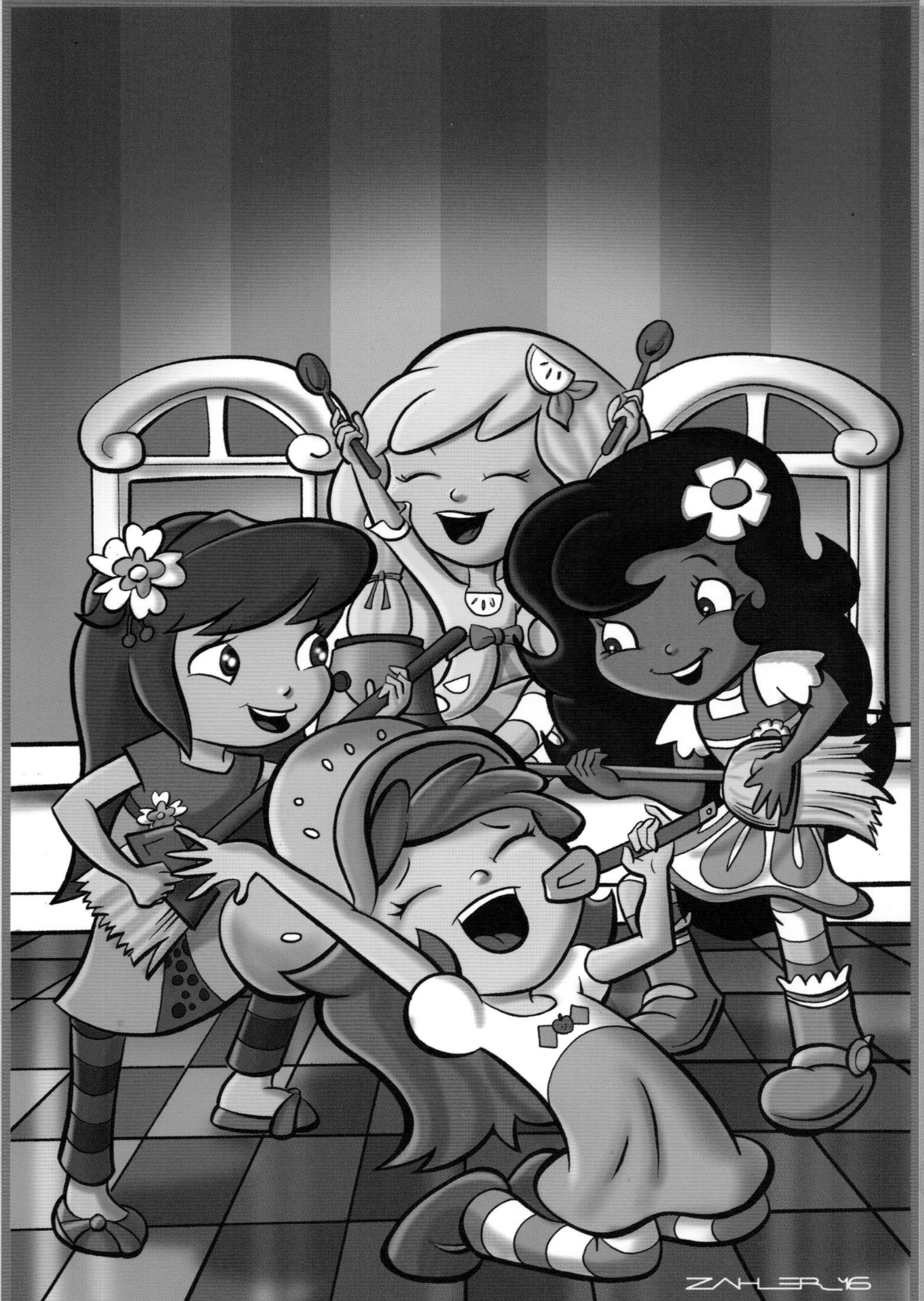
ZAHLER '16

COVER ART BY
Thom Zahler

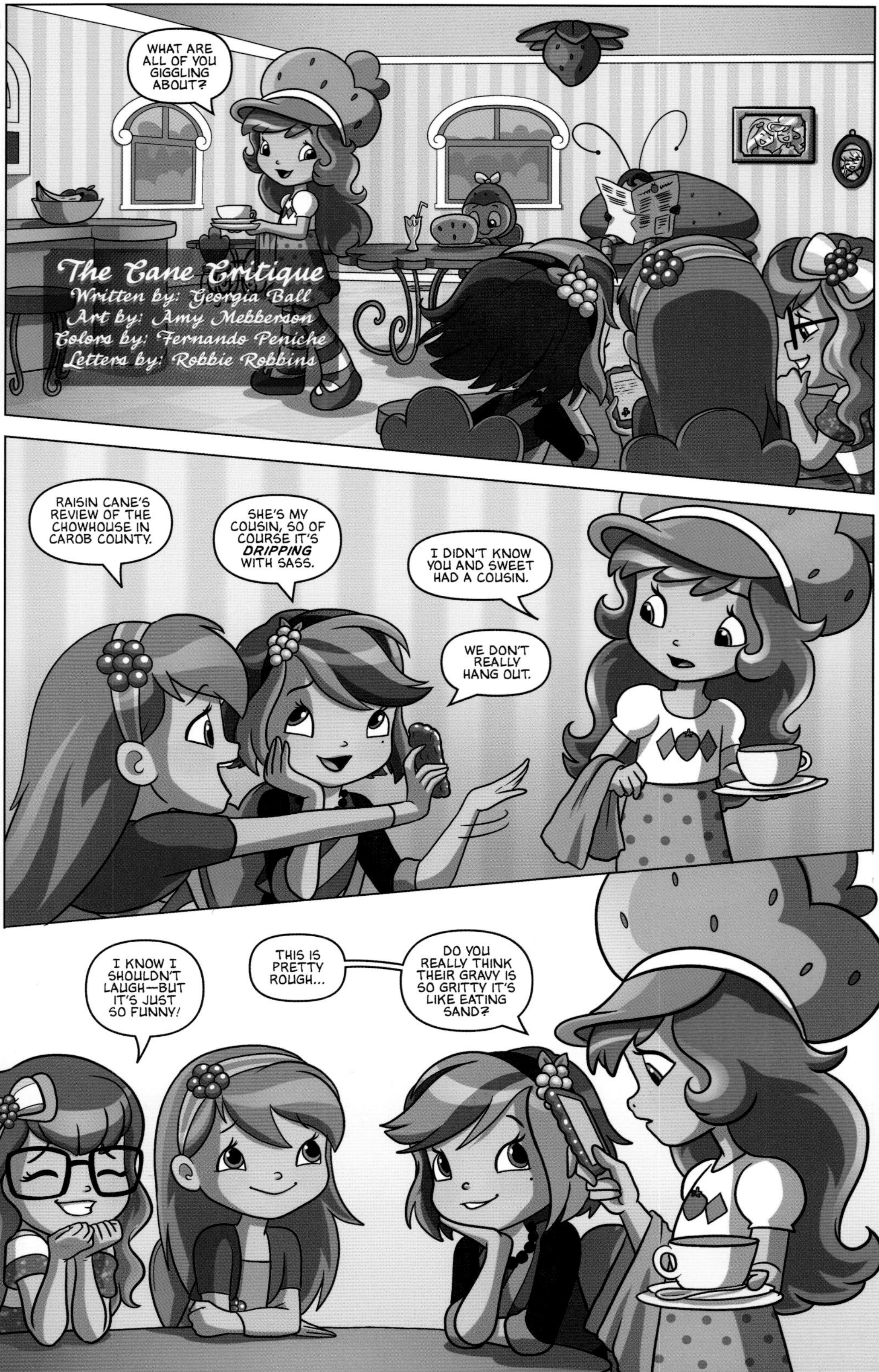
WHAT ARE ALL OF YOU GIGGLING ABOUT?
The Cane Critique
Written by: Georgia Ball
Art by: Amy Mebberson
Colors by: Fernando Peniche
Letters by: Robbie Robbins
RAISIN CANE'S REVIEW OF THE CHOWHOUSE IN CAROB COUNTY.
SHE'S MY COUSIN, SO OF COURSE IT'S ***DRIPPING*** WITH SASS.
I DIDN'T KNOW YOU AND SWEET HAD A COUSIN.
WE DON'T REALLY HANG OUT.
I KNOW I SHOULDN'T LAUGH—BUT IT'S JUST SO FUNNY!
THIS IS PRETTY ROUGH...
DO YOU REALLY THINK THEIR GRAVY IS SO GRITTY IT'S LIKE EATING SAND?

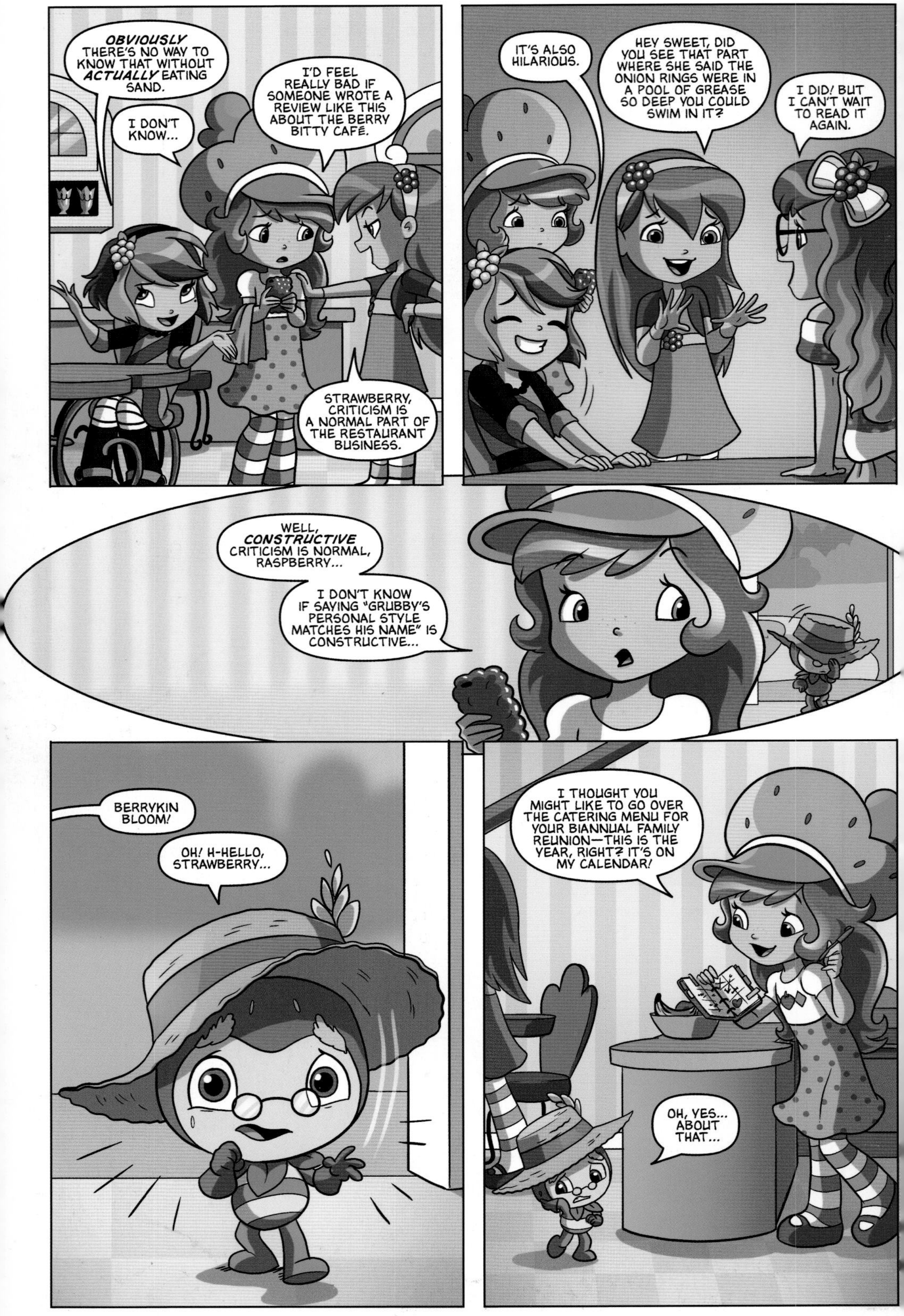

OBVIOUSLY THERE'S NO WAY TO KNOW THAT WITHOUT ACTUALLY EATING SAND.
I DON'T KNOW...
I'D FEEL REALLY BAD IF SOMEONE WROTE A REVIEW LIKE THIS ABOUT THE BERRY BITTY CAFÉ.
STRAWBERRY, CRITICISM IS A NORMAL PART OF THE RESTAURANT BUSINESS.
IT'S ALSO HILARIOUS.
HEY SWEET, DID YOU SEE THAT PART WHERE SHE SAID THE ONION RINGS WERE IN A POOL OF GREASE SO DEEP YOU COULD SWIM IN IT?
I DID! BUT I CAN'T WAIT TO READ IT AGAIN.
WELL, CONSTRUCTIVE CRITICISM IS NORMAL, RASPBERRY...
I DON'T KNOW IF SAYING "GRUBBY'S PERSONAL STYLE MATCHES HIS NAME" IS CONSTRUCTIVE...
BERRYKIN BLOOM!
OH! H-HELLO, STRAWBERRY...
I THOUGHT YOU MIGHT LIKE TO GO OVER THE CATERING MENU FOR YOUR BIANNUAL FAMILY REUNION—THIS IS THE YEAR, RIGHT? IT'S ON MY CALENDAR!
OH, YES... ABOUT THAT...

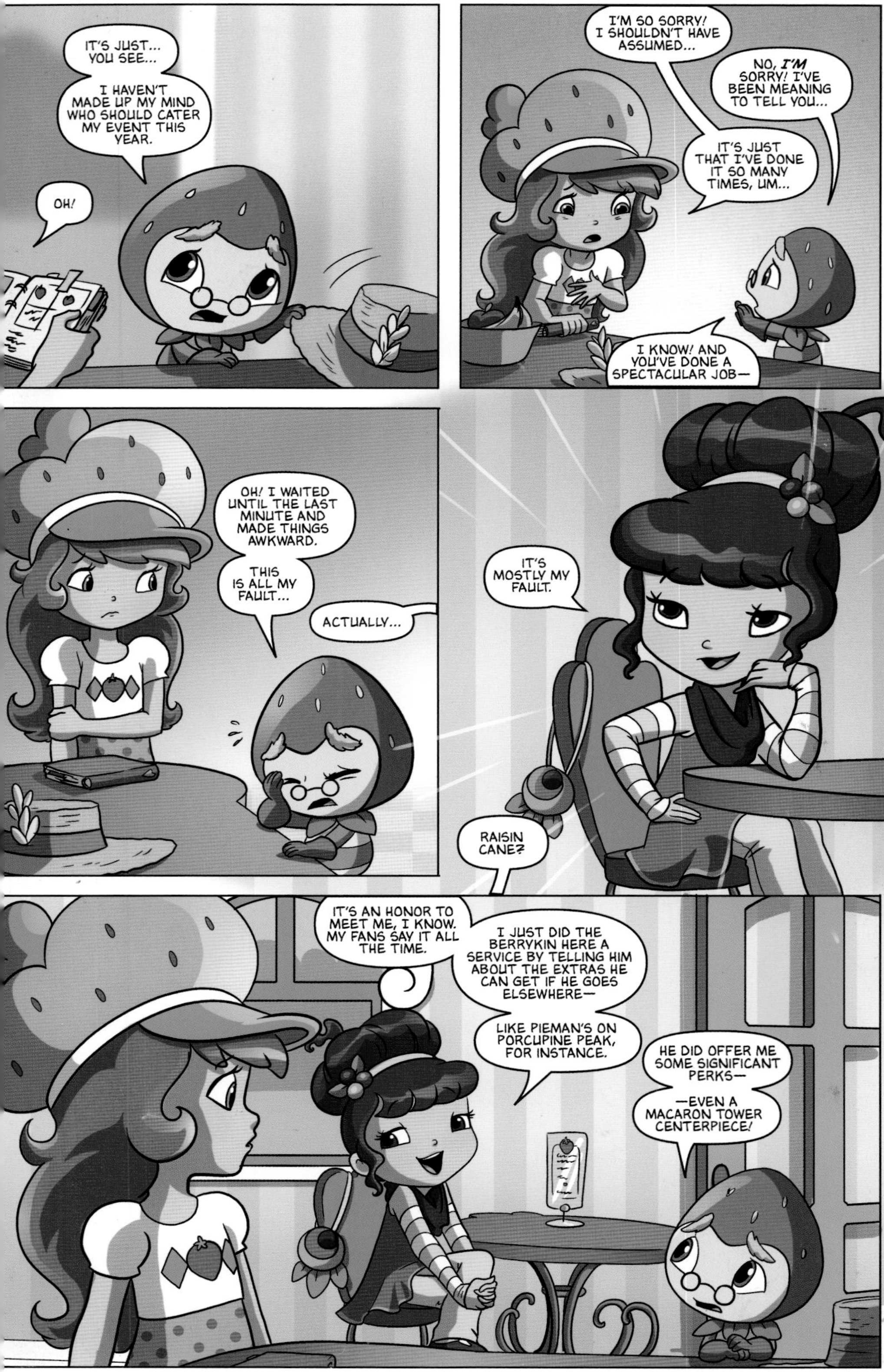
IT'S JUST... YOU SEE...
I HAVEN'T MADE UP MY MIND WHO SHOULD CATER MY EVENT THIS YEAR.
OH!
I'M SO SORRY! I SHOULDN'T HAVE ASSUMED...
NO, I'M SORRY! I'VE BEEN MEANING TO TELL YOU...
IT'S JUST THAT I'VE DONE IT SO MANY TIMES, UM...
I KNOW! AND YOU'VE DONE A SPECTACULAR JOB—
OH! I WAITED UNTIL THE LAST MINUTE AND MADE THINGS AWKWARD.
THIS IS ALL MY FAULT...
ACTUALLY...
IT'S MOSTLY MY FAULT.
RAISIN CANE?
IT'S AN HONOR TO MEET ME, I KNOW. MY FANS SAY IT ALL THE TIME.
I JUST DID THE BERRYKIN HERE A SERVICE BY TELLING HIM ABOUT THE EXTRAS HE CAN GET IF HE GOES ELSEWHERE—
LIKE PIEMAN'S ON PORCUPINE PEAK, FOR INSTANCE.
HE DID OFFER ME SOME SIGNIFICANT PERKS—
—EVEN A MACARON TOWER CENTERPIECE!

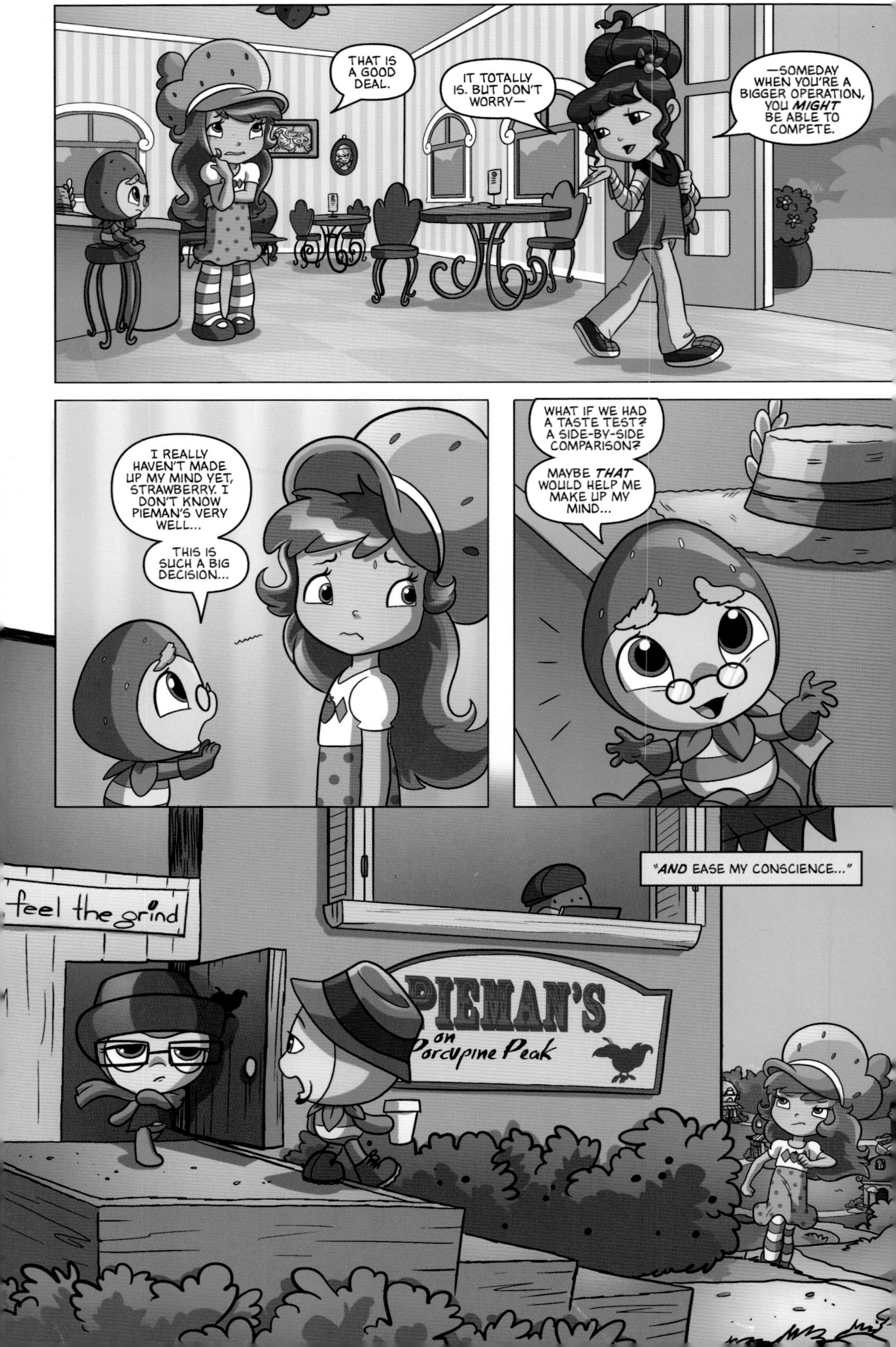
THAT IS A GOOD DEAL.
IT TOTALLY IS. BUT DON'T WORRY—
—SOMEDAY WHEN YOU'RE A BIGGER OPERATION, YOU **MIGHT** BE ABLE TO COMPETE.
I REALLY HAVEN'T MADE UP MY MIND YET, STRAWBERRY. I DON'T KNOW PIEMAN'S VERY WELL...
THIS IS SUCH A BIG DECISION...
WHAT IF WE HAD A TASTE TEST? A SIDE-BY-SIDE COMPARISON?
MAYBE **THAT** WOULD HELP ME MAKE UP MY MIND...
"**AND** EASE MY CONSCIENCE..."
feel the grind
PIEMAN'S on Porcupine Peak

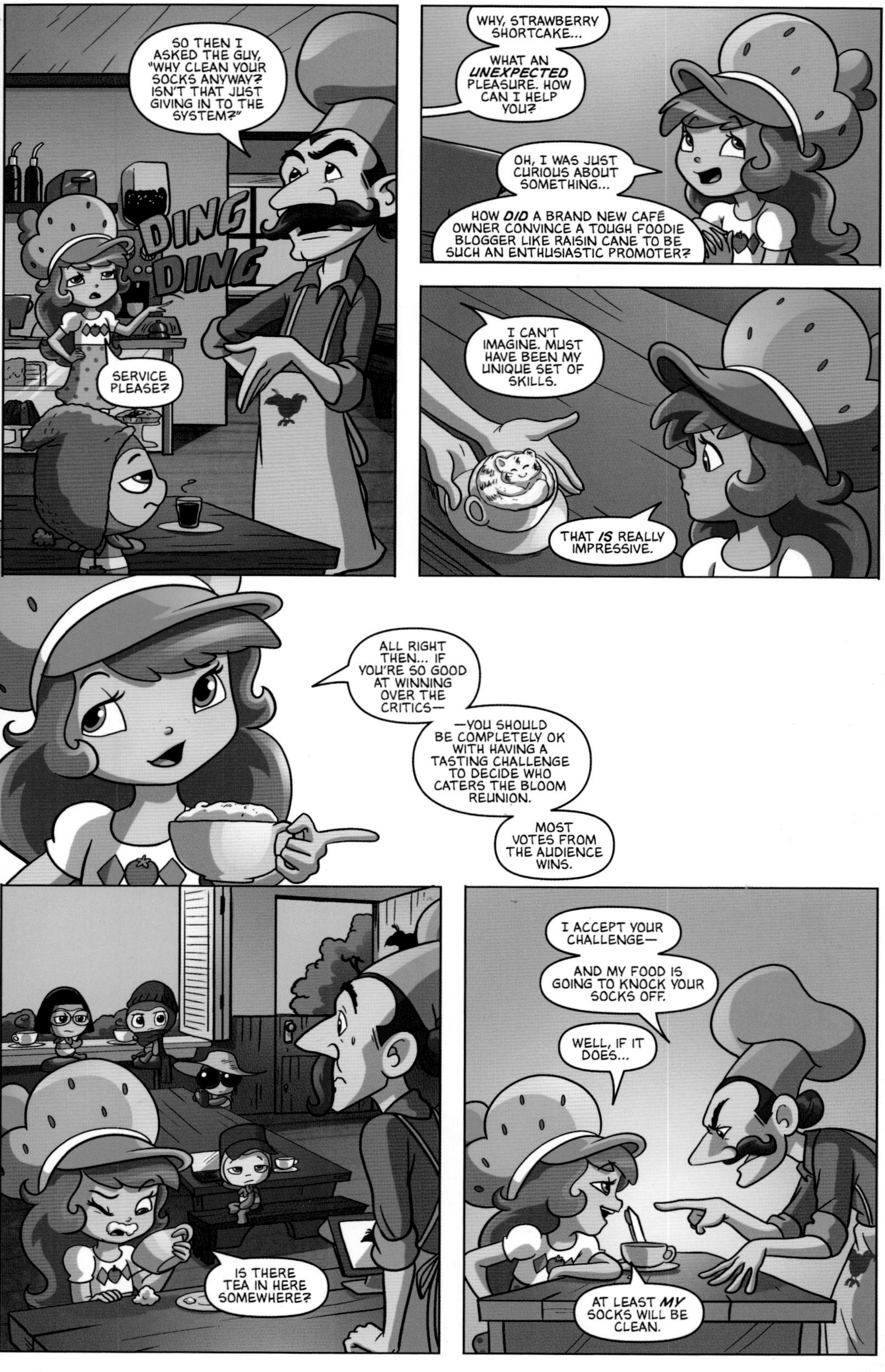

SO THEN I ASKED THE GUY, "WHY CLEAN YOUR SOCKS ANYWAY? ISN'T THAT JUST GIVING IN TO THE SYSTEM?"
DING DING
SERVICE PLEASE?
WHY, STRAWBERRY SHORTCAKE...
WHAT AN *UNEXPECTED* PLEASURE. HOW CAN I HELP YOU?
OH, I WAS JUST CURIOUS ABOUT SOMETHING...
HOW *DID* A BRAND NEW CAFÉ OWNER CONVINCE A TOUGH FOODIE BLOGGER LIKE RAISIN CANE TO BE SUCH AN ENTHUSIASTIC PROMOTER?
I CAN'T IMAGINE. MUST HAVE BEEN MY UNIQUE SET OF SKILLS.
THAT *IS* REALLY IMPRESSIVE.
ALL RIGHT THEN... IF YOU'RE SO GOOD AT WINNING OVER THE CRITICS—
—YOU SHOULD BE COMPLETELY OK WITH HAVING A TASTING CHALLENGE TO DECIDE WHO CATERS THE BLOOM REUNION.
MOST VOTES FROM THE AUDIENCE WINS.
IS THERE TEA IN HERE SOMEWHERE?
I ACCEPT YOUR CHALLENGE—
AND MY FOOD IS GOING TO KNOCK YOUR SOCKS OFF.
WELL, IF IT DOES...
AT LEAST *MY* SOCKS WILL BE CLEAN.

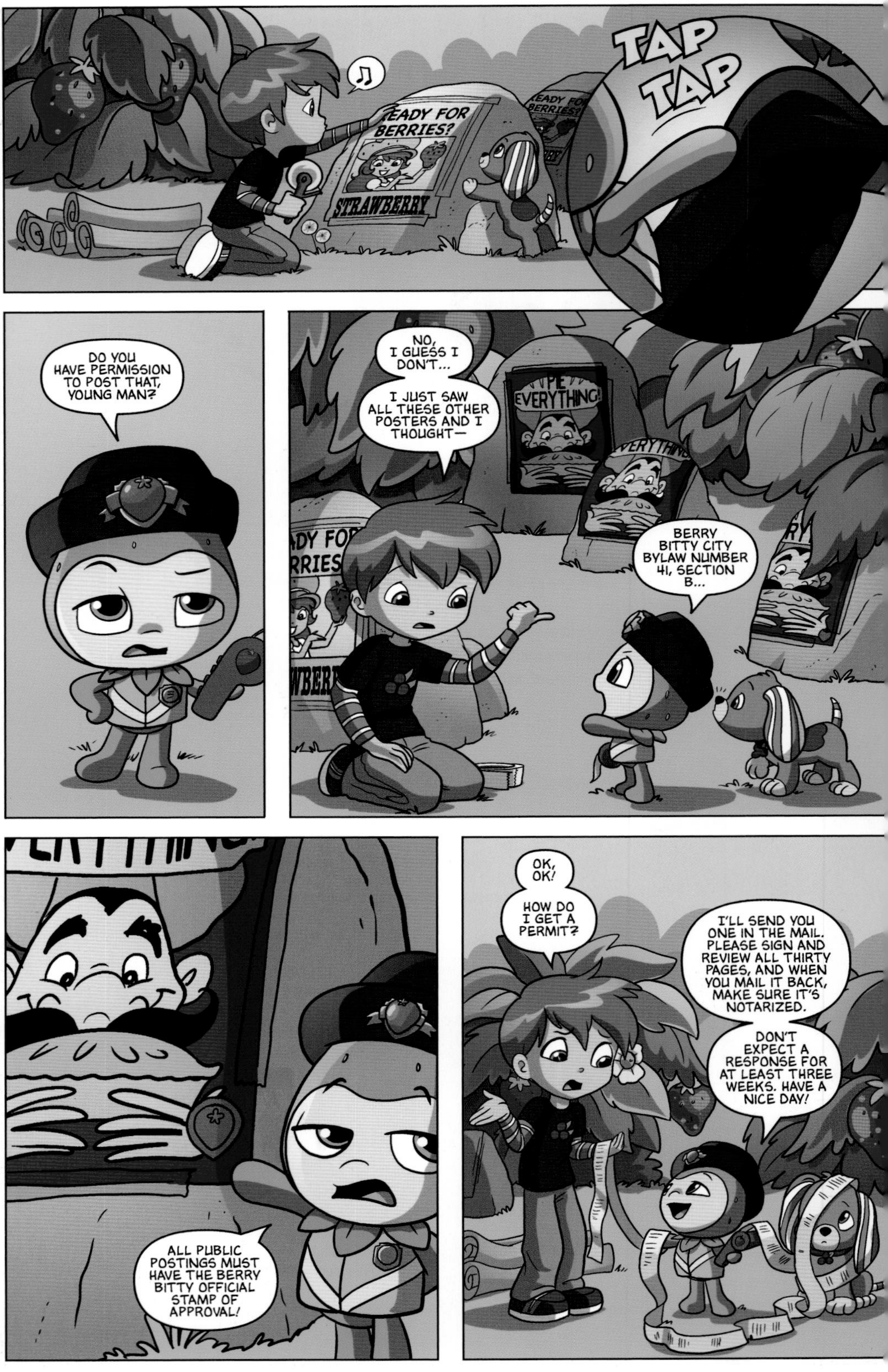
READY FOR BERRIES?
STRAWBERRY
♫
TAP TAP
DO YOU HAVE PERMISSION TO POST THAT, YOUNG MAN?
NO, I GUESS I DON'T...
I JUST SAW ALL THESE OTHER POSTERS AND I THOUGHT—
PIE EVERYTHING!
BERRY BITTY CITY BYLAW NUMBER 41, SECTION B...
ALL PUBLIC POSTINGS MUST HAVE THE BERRY BITTY OFFICIAL STAMP OF APPROVAL!
OK, OK!
HOW DO I GET A PERMIT?
I'LL SEND YOU ONE IN THE MAIL. PLEASE SIGN AND REVIEW ALL THIRTY PAGES, AND WHEN YOU MAIL IT BACK, MAKE SURE IT'S NOTARIZED.
DON'T EXPECT A RESPONSE FOR AT LEAST THREE WEEKS. HAVE A NICE DAY!

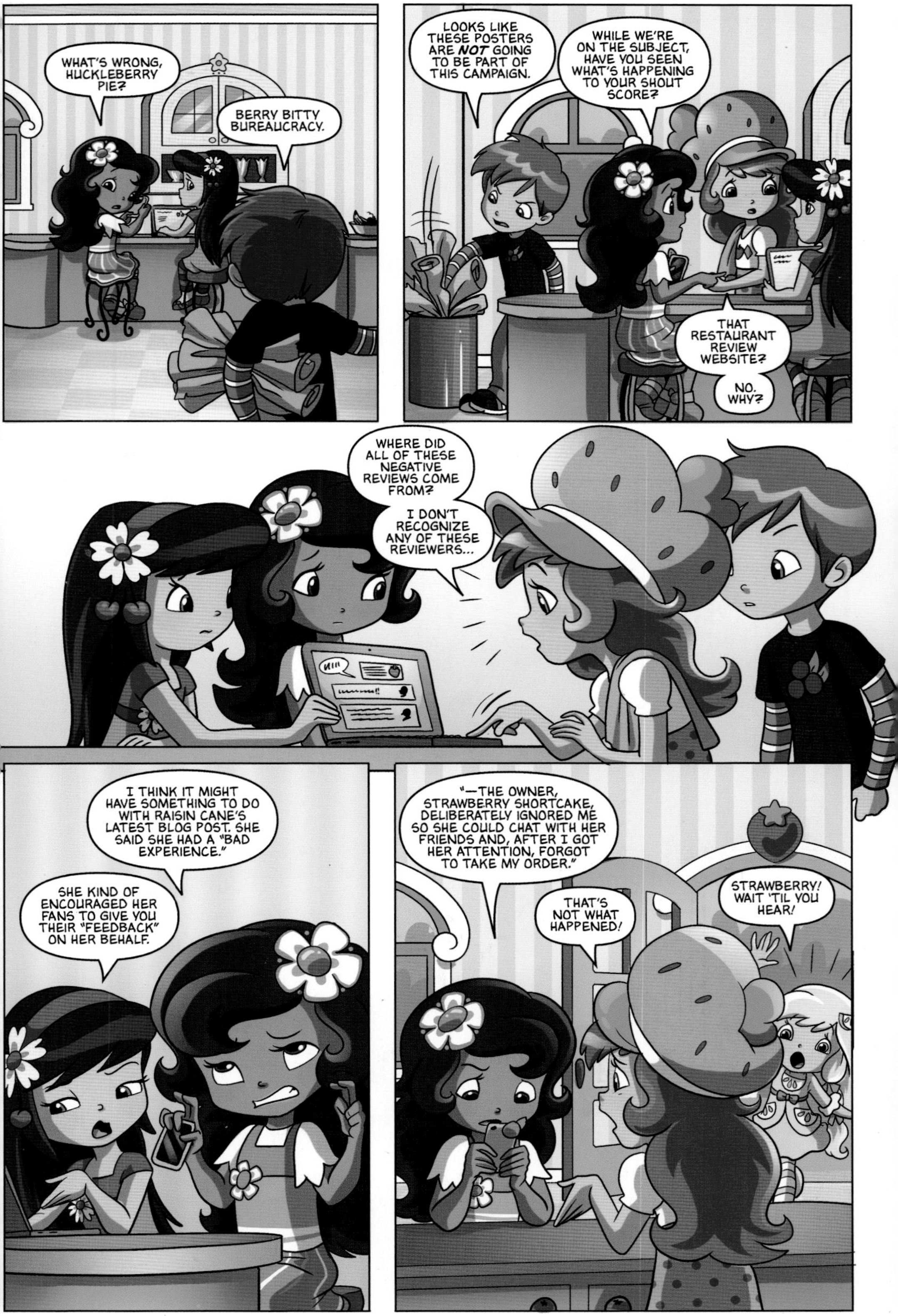
WHAT'S WRONG, HUCKLEBERRY PIE?
BERRY BITTY BUREAUCRACY.
LOOKS LIKE THESE POSTERS ARE *NOT* GOING TO BE PART OF THIS CAMPAIGN.
WHILE WE'RE ON THE SUBJECT, HAVE YOU SEEN WHAT'S HAPPENING TO YOUR SHOUT SCORE?
THAT RESTAURANT REVIEW WEBSITE?
NO. WHY?
WHERE DID ALL OF THESE NEGATIVE REVIEWS COME FROM?
I DON'T RECOGNIZE ANY OF THESE REVIEWERS...
I THINK IT MIGHT HAVE SOMETHING TO DO WITH RAISIN CANE'S LATEST BLOG POST. SHE SAID SHE HAD A "BAD EXPERIENCE."
SHE KIND OF ENCOURAGED HER FANS TO GIVE YOU THEIR "FEEDBACK" ON HER BEHALF.
"—THE OWNER, STRAWBERRY SHORTCAKE, DELIBERATELY IGNORED ME SO SHE COULD CHAT WITH HER FRIENDS AND, AFTER I GOT HER ATTENTION, FORGOT TO TAKE MY ORDER."
THAT'S NOT WHAT HAPPENED!
STRAWBERRY! WAIT 'TIL YOU HEAR!

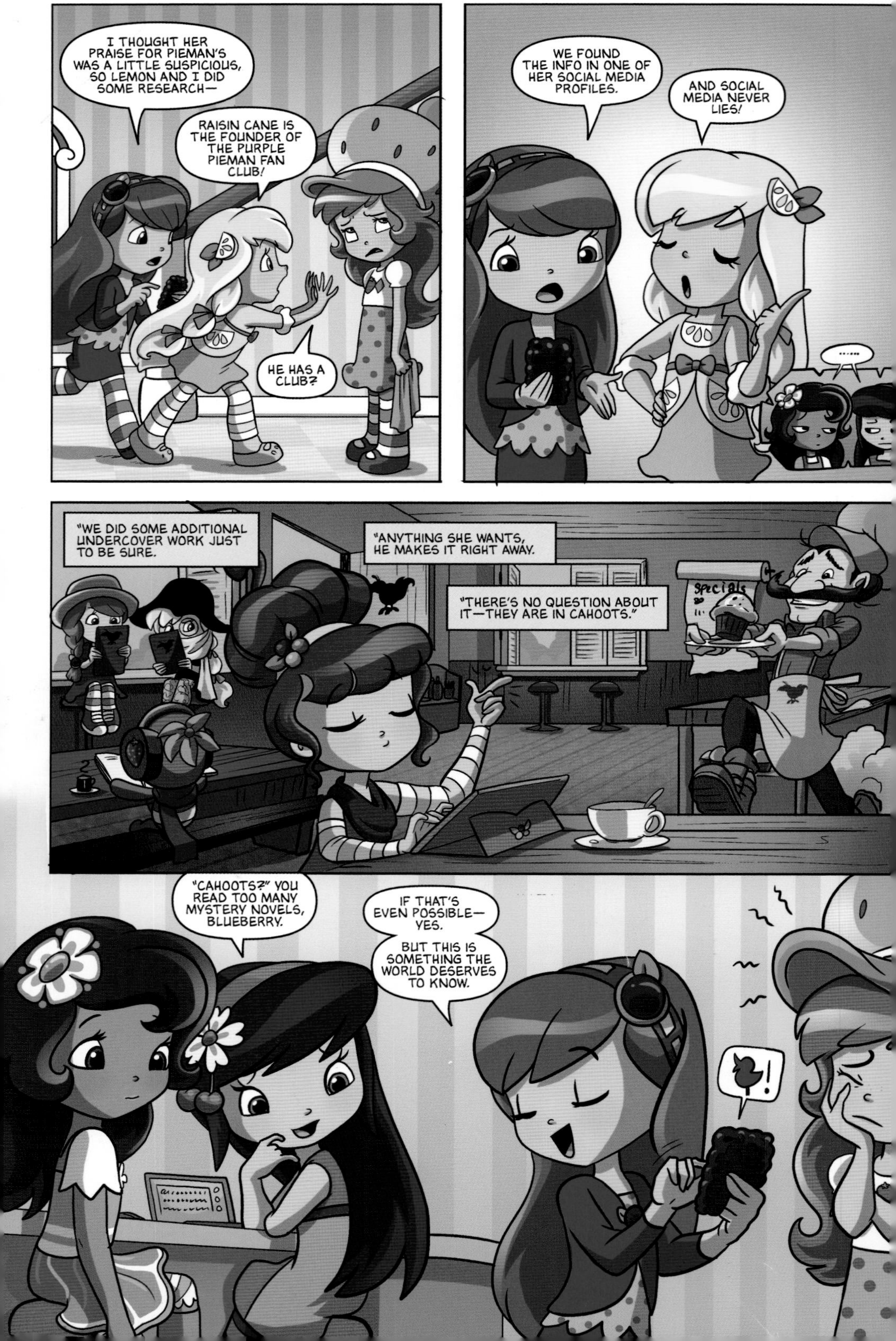
I THOUGHT HER PRAISE FOR PIEMAN'S WAS A LITTLE SUSPICIOUS, SO LEMON AND I DID SOME RESEARCH—
RAISIN CANE IS THE FOUNDER OF THE PURPLE PIEMAN FAN CLUB!
HE HAS A CLUB?
WE FOUND THE INFO IN ONE OF HER SOCIAL MEDIA PROFILES.
AND SOCIAL MEDIA NEVER LIES!
.....
"WE DID SOME ADDITIONAL UNDERCOVER WORK JUST TO BE SURE.
"ANYTHING SHE WANTS, HE MAKES IT RIGHT AWAY.
"THERE'S NO QUESTION ABOUT IT—THEY ARE IN CAHOOTS."
Specials
"CAHOOTS?" YOU READ TOO MANY MYSTERY NOVELS, BLUEBERRY.
IF THAT'S EVEN POSSIBLE—YES.
BUT THIS IS SOMETHING THE WORLD DESERVES TO KNOW.
!

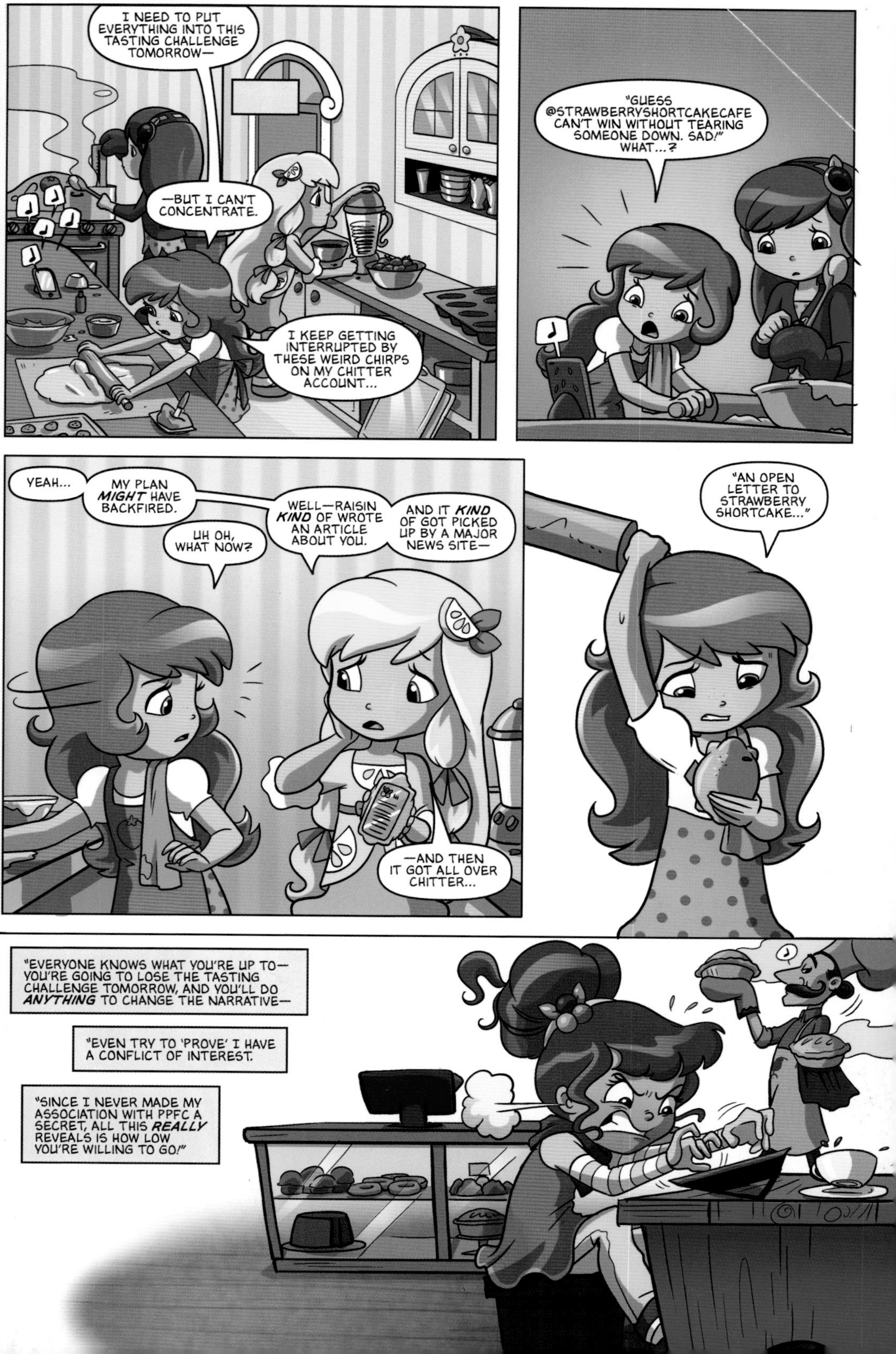

I NEED TO PUT EVERYTHING INTO THIS TASTING CHALLENGE TOMORROW—
—BUT I CAN'T CONCENTRATE.
I KEEP GETTING INTERRUPTED BY THESE WEIRD CHIRPS ON MY CHITTER ACCOUNT...
"GUESS @STRAWBERRYSHORTCAKECAFE CAN'T WIN WITHOUT TEARING SOMEONE DOWN. SAD!" WHAT...?
YEAH...
MY PLAN *MIGHT* HAVE BACKFIRED.
UH OH, WHAT NOW?
WELL—RAISIN *KIND* OF WROTE AN ARTICLE ABOUT YOU.
AND IT *KIND* OF GOT PICKED UP BY A MAJOR NEWS SITE—
—AND THEN IT GOT ALL OVER CHITTER...
"AN OPEN LETTER TO STRAWBERRY SHORTCAKE..."
"EVERYONE KNOWS WHAT YOU'RE UP TO—YOU'RE GOING TO LOSE THE TASTING CHALLENGE TOMORROW, AND YOU'LL DO *ANYTHING* TO CHANGE THE NARRATIVE—
"EVEN TRY TO 'PROVE' I HAVE A CONFLICT OF INTEREST.
"SINCE I NEVER MADE MY ASSOCIATION WITH PPFC A SECRET, ALL THIS *REALLY* REVEALS IS HOW LOW YOU'RE WILLING TO GO!"

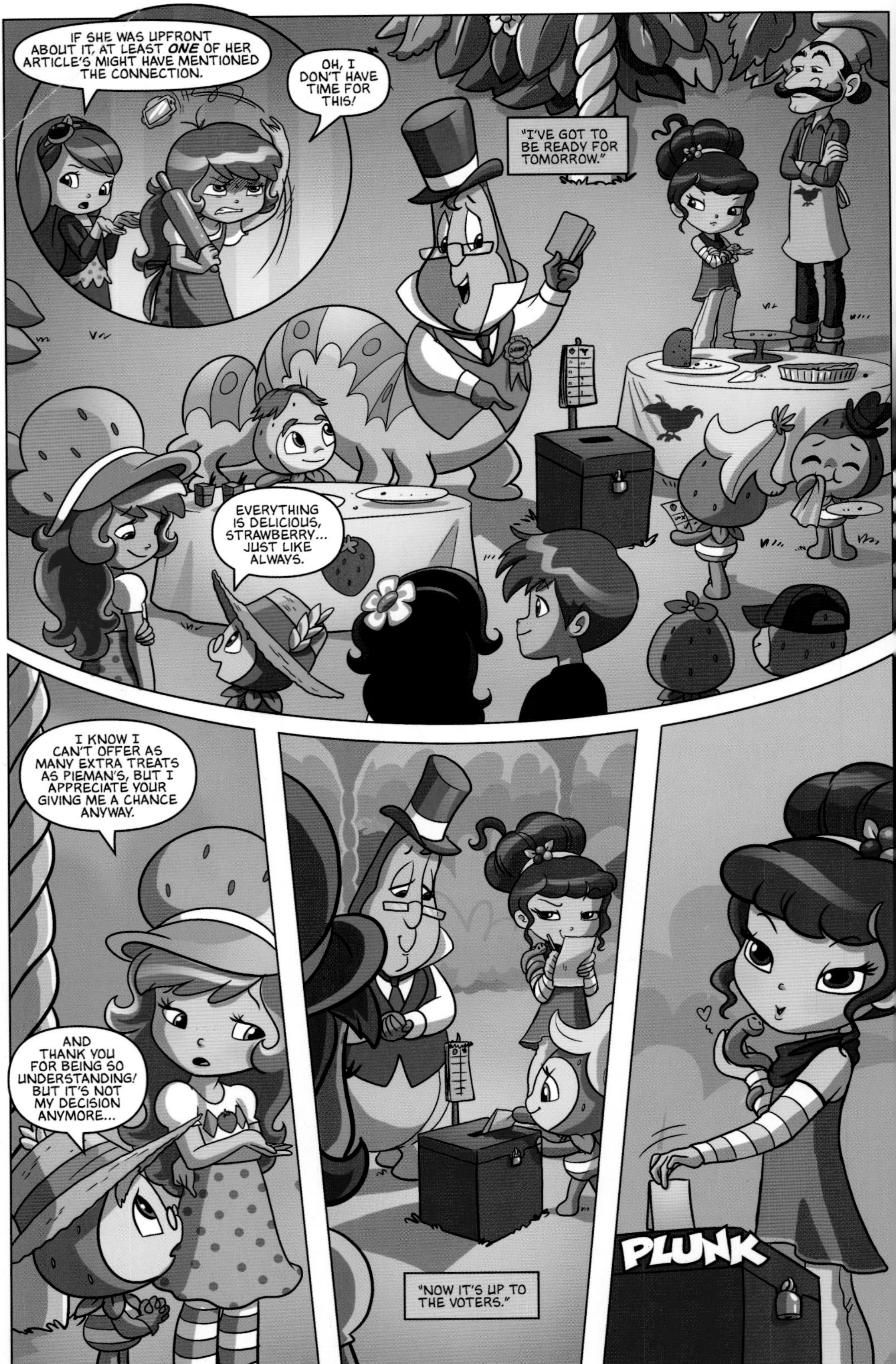
IF SHE WAS UPFRONT ABOUT IT, AT LEAST *ONE* OF HER ARTICLE'S MIGHT HAVE MENTIONED THE CONNECTION.
OH, I DON'T HAVE TIME FOR THIS!
"I'VE GOT TO BE READY FOR TOMORROW."
EVERYTHING IS DELICIOUS, STRAWBERRY... JUST LIKE ALWAYS.
I KNOW I CAN'T OFFER AS MANY EXTRA TREATS AS PIEMAN'S, BUT I APPRECIATE YOUR GIVING ME A CHANCE ANYWAY.
AND THANK YOU FOR BEING SO UNDERSTANDING! BUT IT'S NOT MY DECISION ANYMORE...
"NOW IT'S UP TO THE VOTERS."
PLUNK

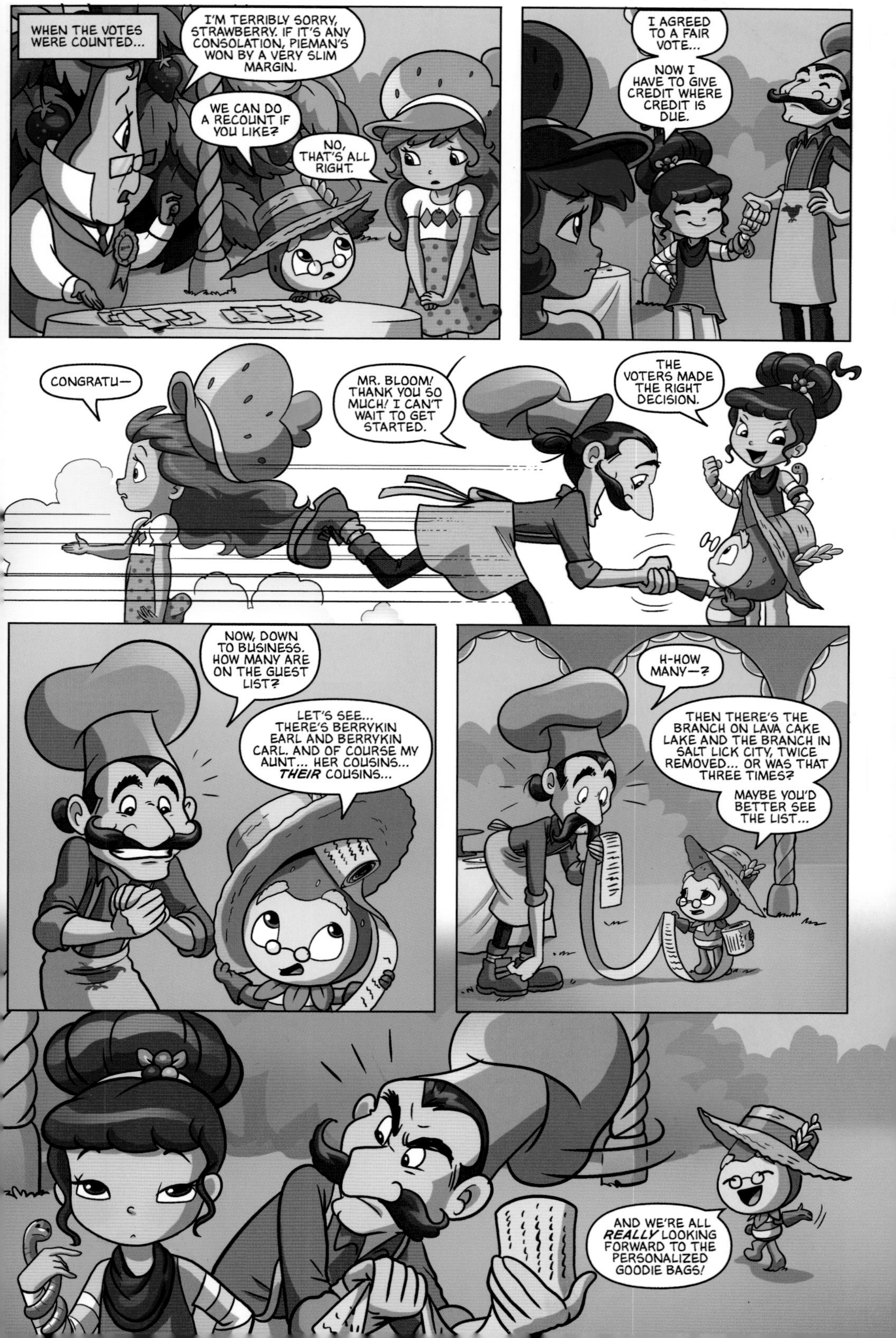
WHEN THE VOTES WERE COUNTED...
I'M TERRIBLY SORRY, STRAWBERRY. IF IT'S ANY CONSOLATION, PIEMAN'S WON BY A VERY SLIM MARGIN.
WE CAN DO A RECOUNT IF YOU LIKE?
NO, THAT'S ALL RIGHT.
I AGREED TO A FAIR VOTE...
NOW I HAVE TO GIVE CREDIT WHERE CREDIT IS DUE.
CONGRATU—
MR. BLOOM! THANK YOU SO MUCH! I CAN'T WAIT TO GET STARTED.
THE VOTERS MADE THE RIGHT DECISION.
NOW, DOWN TO BUSINESS. HOW MANY ARE ON THE GUEST LIST?
LET'S SEE... THERE'S BERRYKIN EARL AND BERRYKIN CARL. AND OF COURSE MY AUNT... HER COUSINS... *THEIR* COUSINS...
H-HOW MANY—?
THEN THERE'S THE BRANCH ON LAVA CAKE LAKE AND THE BRANCH IN SALT LICK CITY, TWICE REMOVED... OR WAS THAT THREE TIMES?
MAYBE YOU'D BETTER SEE THE LIST...
AND WE'RE ALL *REALLY* LOOKING FORWARD TO THE PERSONALIZED GOODIE BAGS!

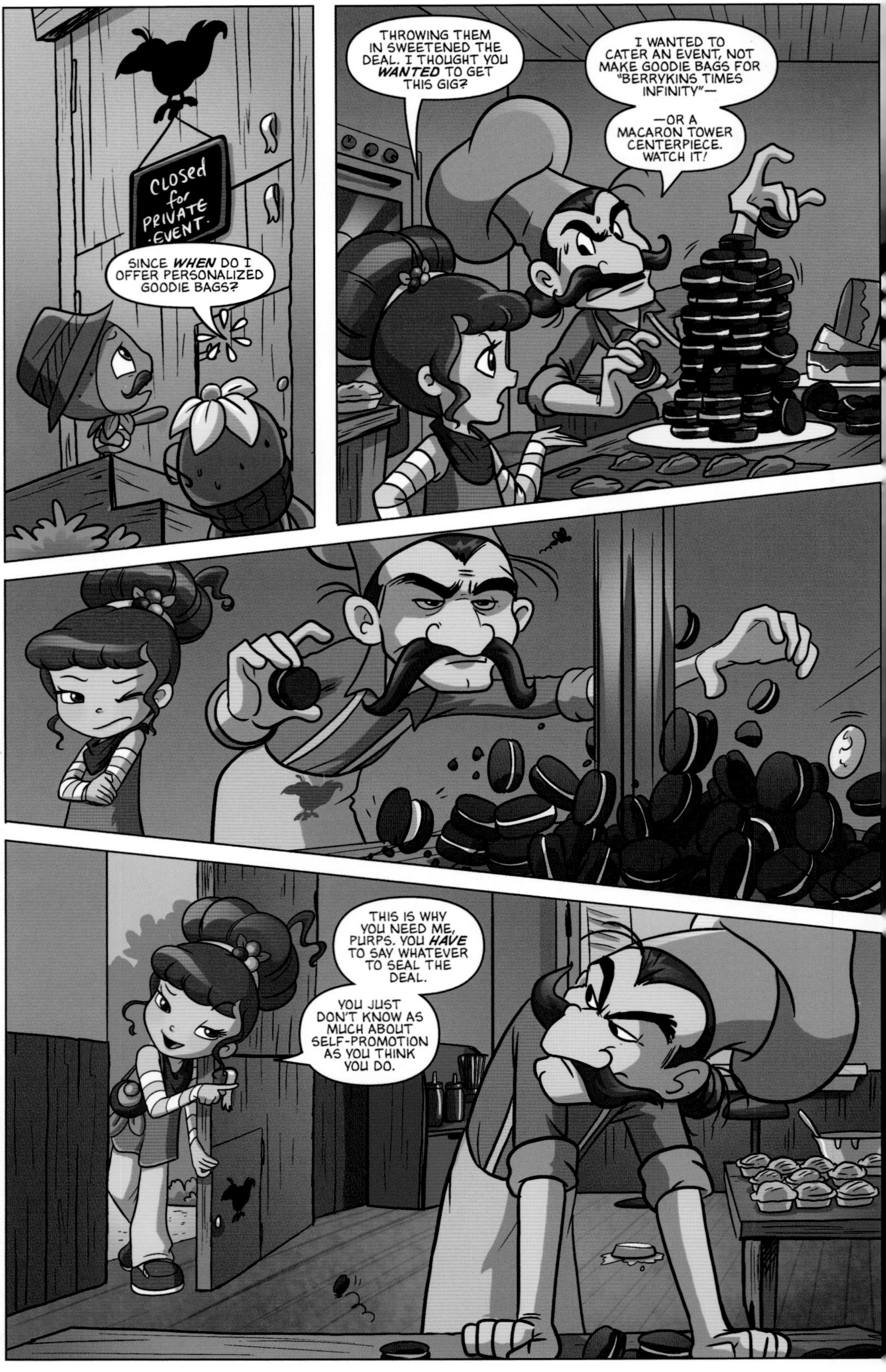
CLOSED for PRIVATE EVENT.
SINCE WHEN DO I OFFER PERSONALIZED GOODIE BAGS?
THROWING THEM IN SWEETENED THE DEAL. I THOUGHT YOU WANTED TO GET THIS GIG?
I WANTED TO CATER AN EVENT, NOT MAKE GOODIE BAGS FOR "BERRYKINS TIMES INFINITY"—
—OR A MACARON TOWER CENTERPIECE. WATCH IT!
THIS IS WHY YOU NEED ME, PURPS. YOU HAVE TO SAY WHATEVER TO SEAL THE DEAL.
YOU JUST DON'T KNOW AS MUCH ABOUT SELF-PROMOTION AS YOU THINK YOU DO.

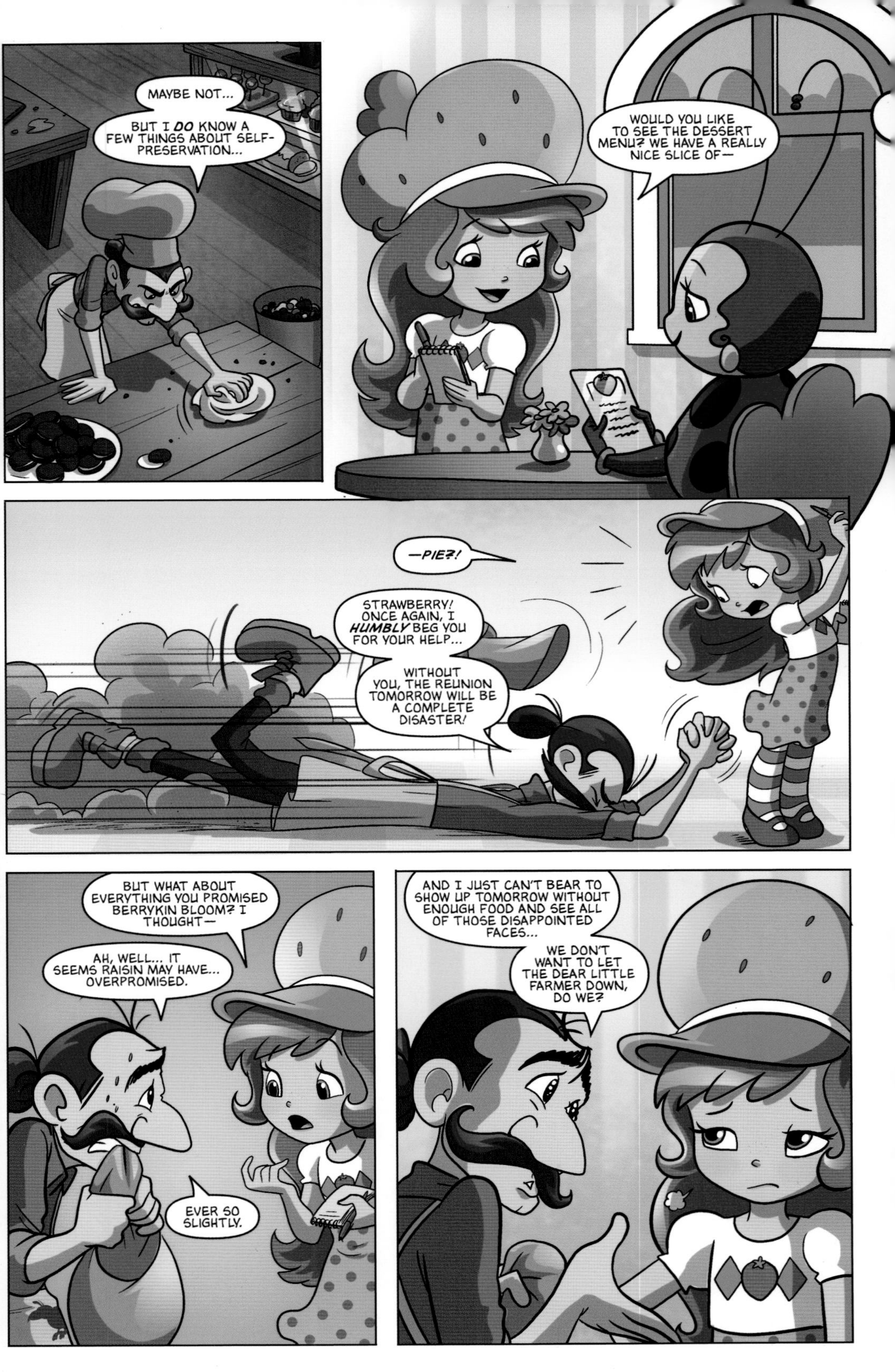
MAYBE NOT...
BUT I **DO** KNOW A FEW THINGS ABOUT SELF-PRESERVATION...
WOULD YOU LIKE TO SEE THE DESSERT MENU? WE HAVE A REALLY NICE SLICE OF—
—PIE?!
STRAWBERRY! ONCE AGAIN, I **HUMBLY** BEG YOU FOR YOUR HELP...
WITHOUT YOU, THE REUNION TOMORROW WILL BE A COMPLETE DISASTER!
BUT WHAT ABOUT EVERYTHING YOU PROMISED BERRYKIN BLOOM? I THOUGHT—
AH, WELL... IT SEEMS RAISIN MAY HAVE... OVERPROMISED.
EVER SO SLIGHTLY.
AND I JUST CAN'T BEAR TO SHOW UP TOMORROW WITHOUT ENOUGH FOOD AND SEE ALL OF THOSE DISAPPOINTED FACES...
WE DON'T WANT TO LET THE DEAR LITTLE FARMER DOWN, DO WE?

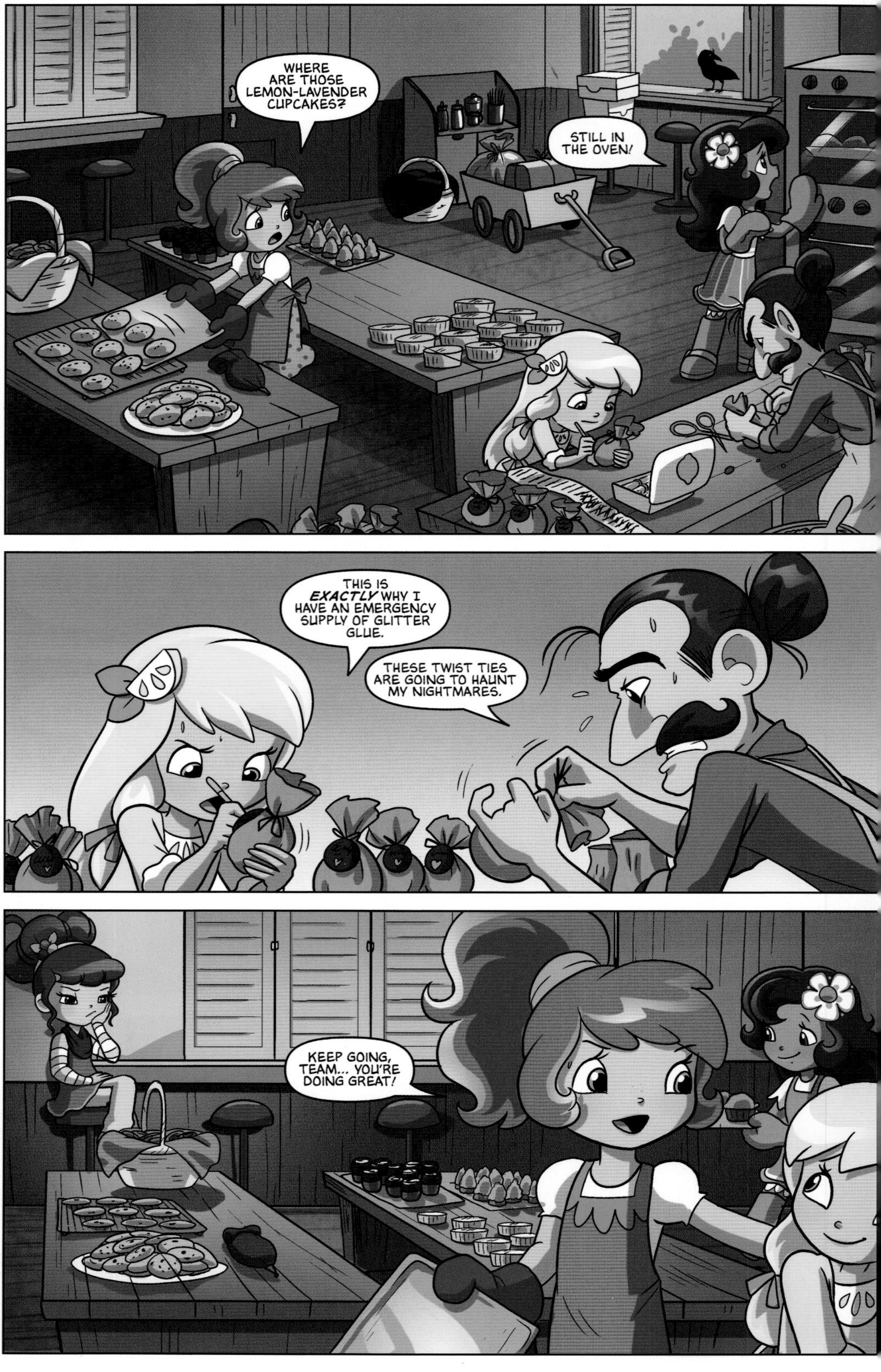
WHERE ARE THOSE LEMON-LAVENDER CUPCAKES?
STILL IN THE OVEN!
THIS IS *EXACTLY* WHY I HAVE AN EMERGENCY SUPPLY OF GLITTER GLUE.
THESE TWIST TIES ARE GOING TO HAUNT MY NIGHTMARES.
KEEP GOING, TEAM... YOU'RE DOING GREAT!

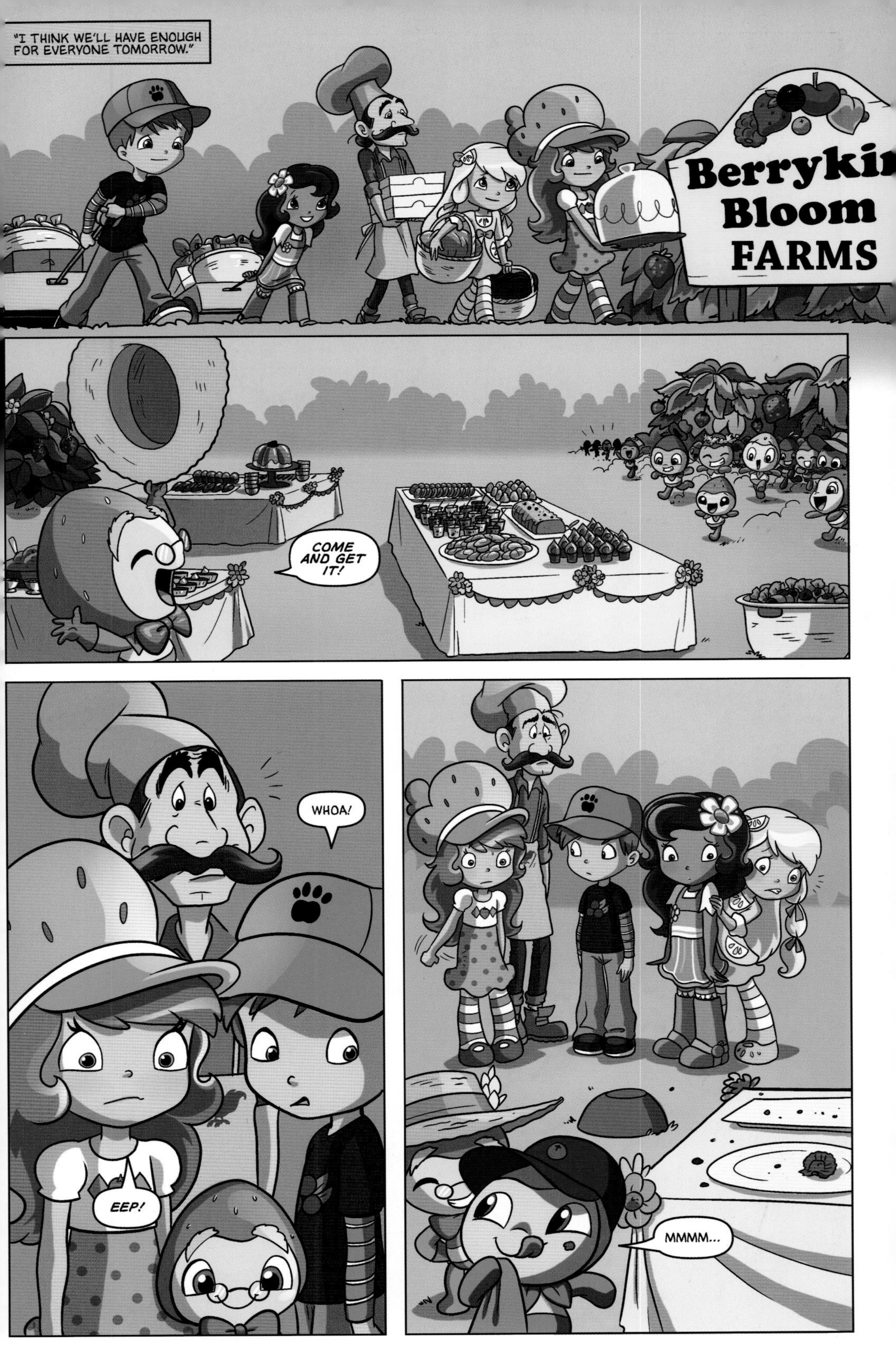
"I THINK WE'LL HAVE ENOUGH FOR EVERYONE TOMORROW."
Berrykin Bloom FARMS
COME AND GET IT!
WHOA!
EEP!
MMMM...

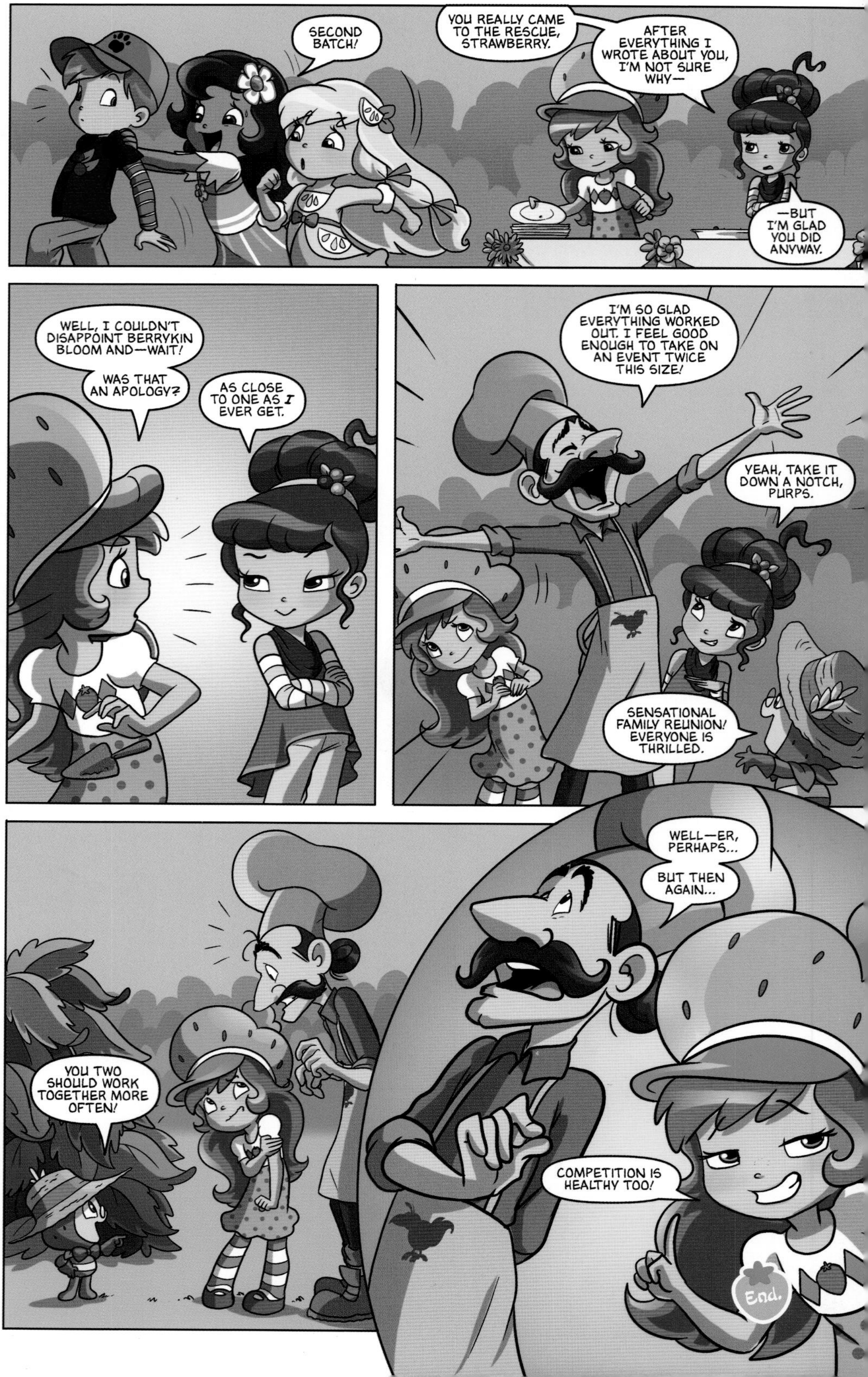

SECOND BATCH!
YOU REALLY CAME TO THE RESCUE, STRAWBERRY.
AFTER EVERYTHING I WROTE ABOUT YOU, I'M NOT SURE WHY—
—BUT I'M GLAD YOU DID ANYWAY.
WELL, I COULDN'T DISAPPOINT BERRYKIN BLOOM AND—WAIT!
WAS THAT AN APOLOGY?
AS CLOSE TO ONE AS I EVER GET.
I'M SO GLAD EVERYTHING WORKED OUT. I FEEL GOOD ENOUGH TO TAKE ON AN EVENT TWICE THIS SIZE!
YEAH, TAKE IT DOWN A NOTCH, PURPS.
SENSATIONAL FAMILY REUNION! EVERYONE IS THRILLED.
YOU TWO SHOULD WORK TOGETHER MORE OFTEN!
WELL—ER, PERHAPS...
BUT THEN AGAIN...
COMPETITION IS HEALTHY TOO!
End.

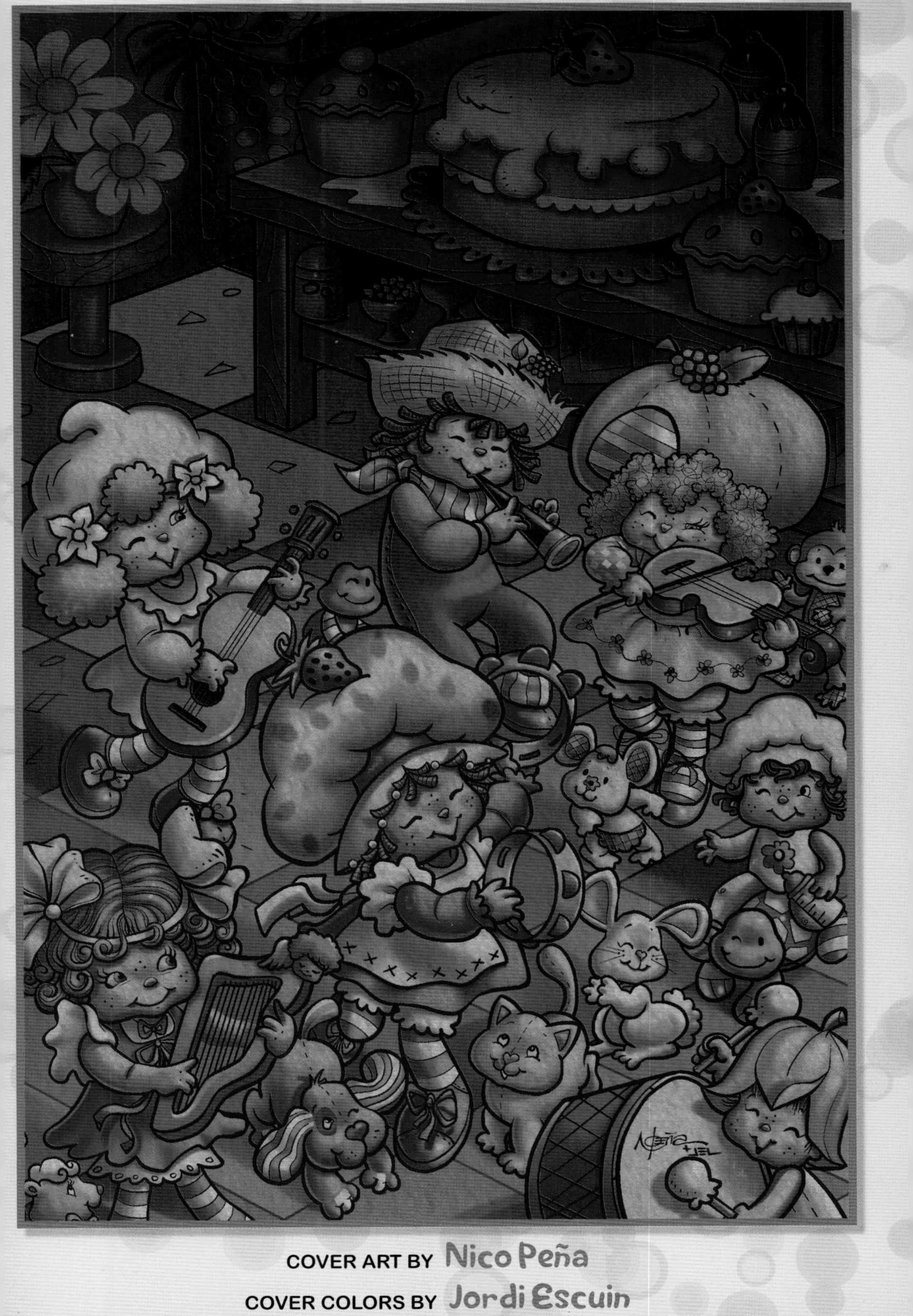

COVER ART BY **Nico Peña**

COVER COLORS BY **Jordi Escuin**

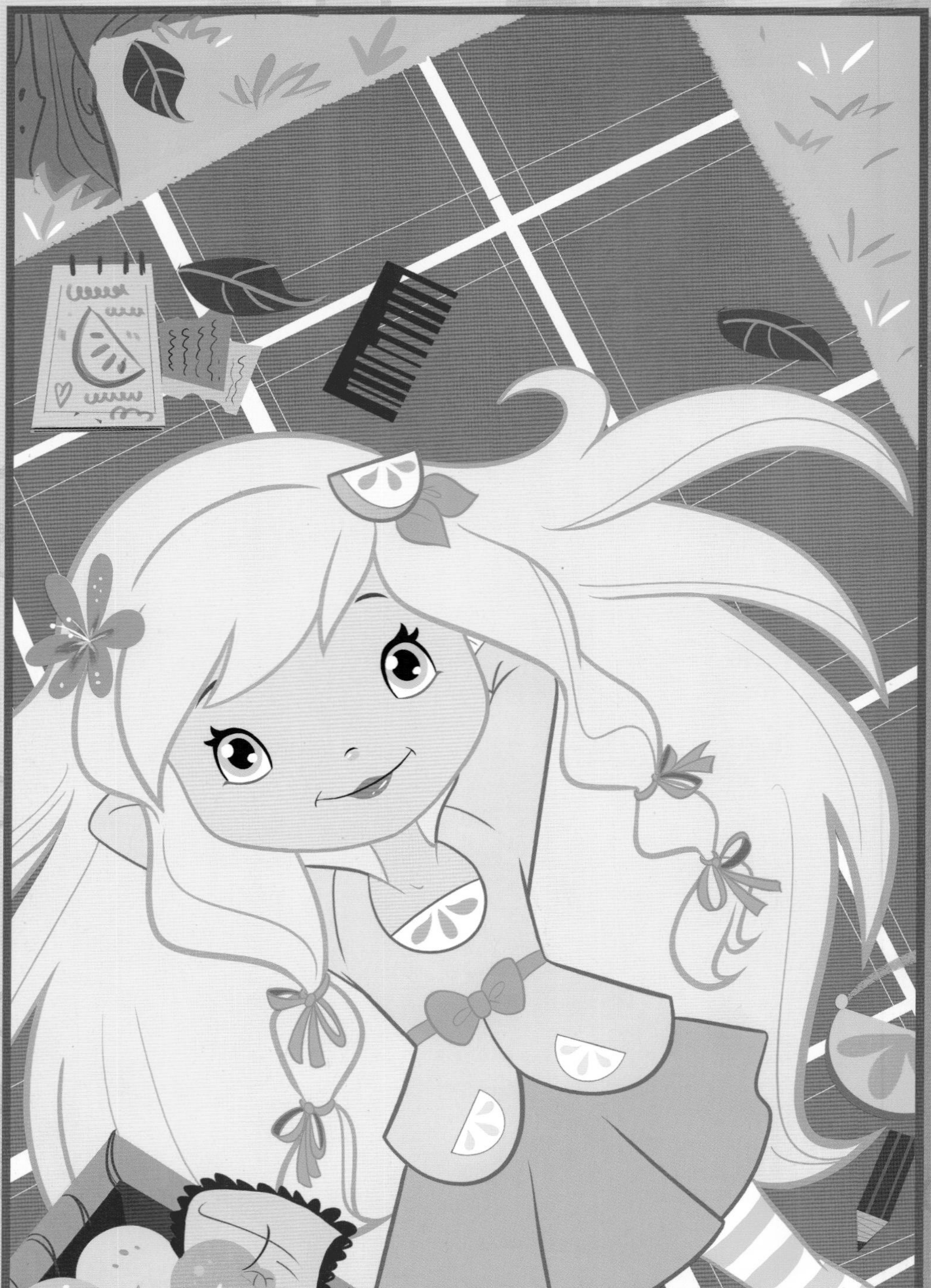

COVER ART BY
Nicoletta Baldari

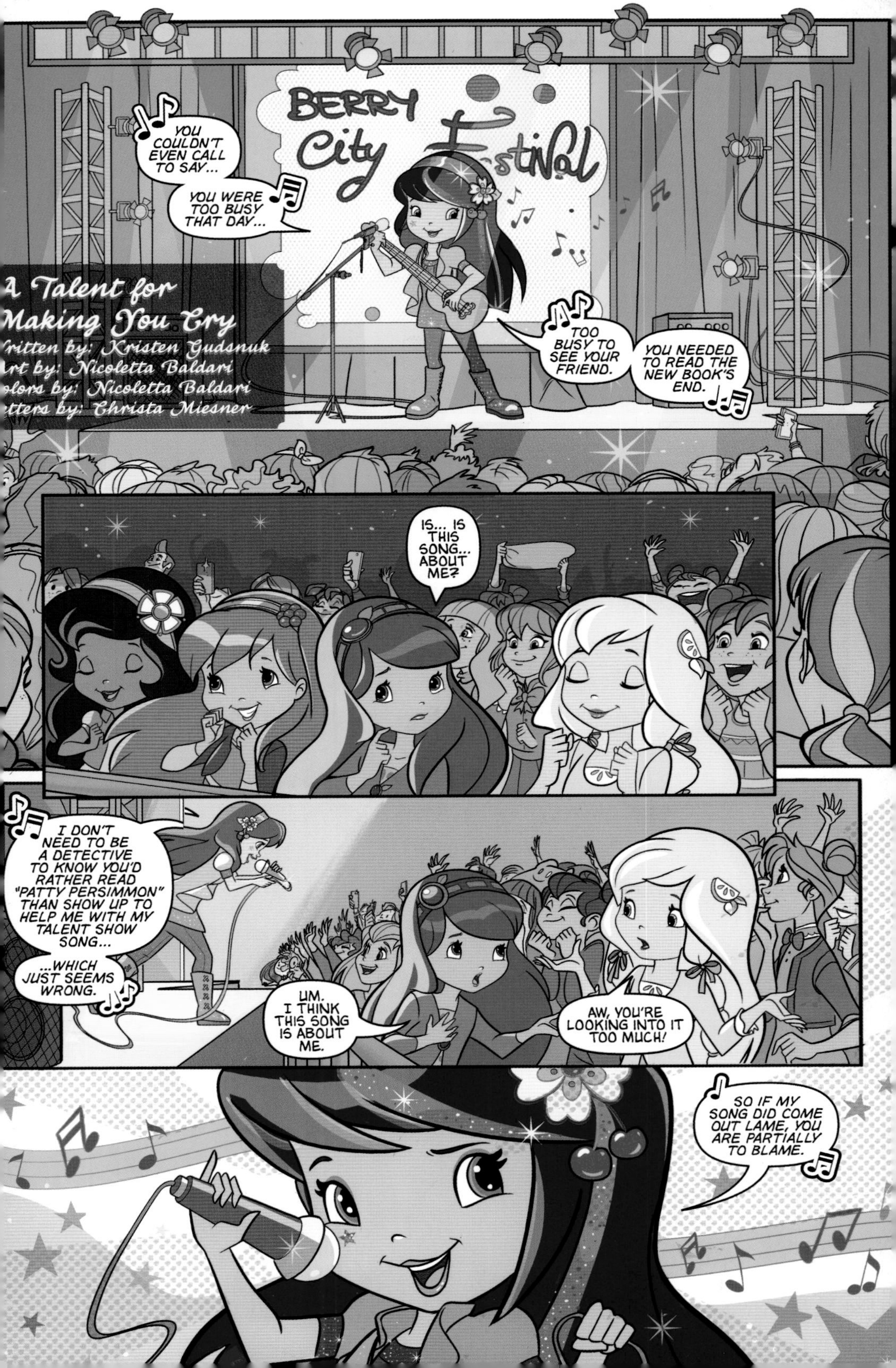
BERRY City Festival
YOU COULDN'T EVEN CALL TO SAY...
YOU WERE TOO BUSY THAT DAY...
A Talent for Making You Cry
Written by: Kristen Gudsnuk
Art by: Nicoletta Baldari
Colors by: Nicoletta Baldari
Letters by: Christa Miesner
TOO BUSY TO SEE YOUR FRIEND.
YOU NEEDED TO READ THE NEW BOOK'S END.
IS... IS THIS SONG... ABOUT ME?
I DON'T NEED TO BE A DETECTIVE TO KNOW YOU'D RATHER READ "PATTY PERSIMMON" THAN SHOW UP TO HELP ME WITH MY TALENT SHOW SONG...
...WHICH JUST SEEMS WRONG.
UM. I THINK THIS SONG IS ABOUT ME.
AW, YOU'RE LOOKING INTO IT TOO MUCH!
SO IF MY SONG DID COME OUT LAME, YOU ARE PARTIALLY TO BLAME.

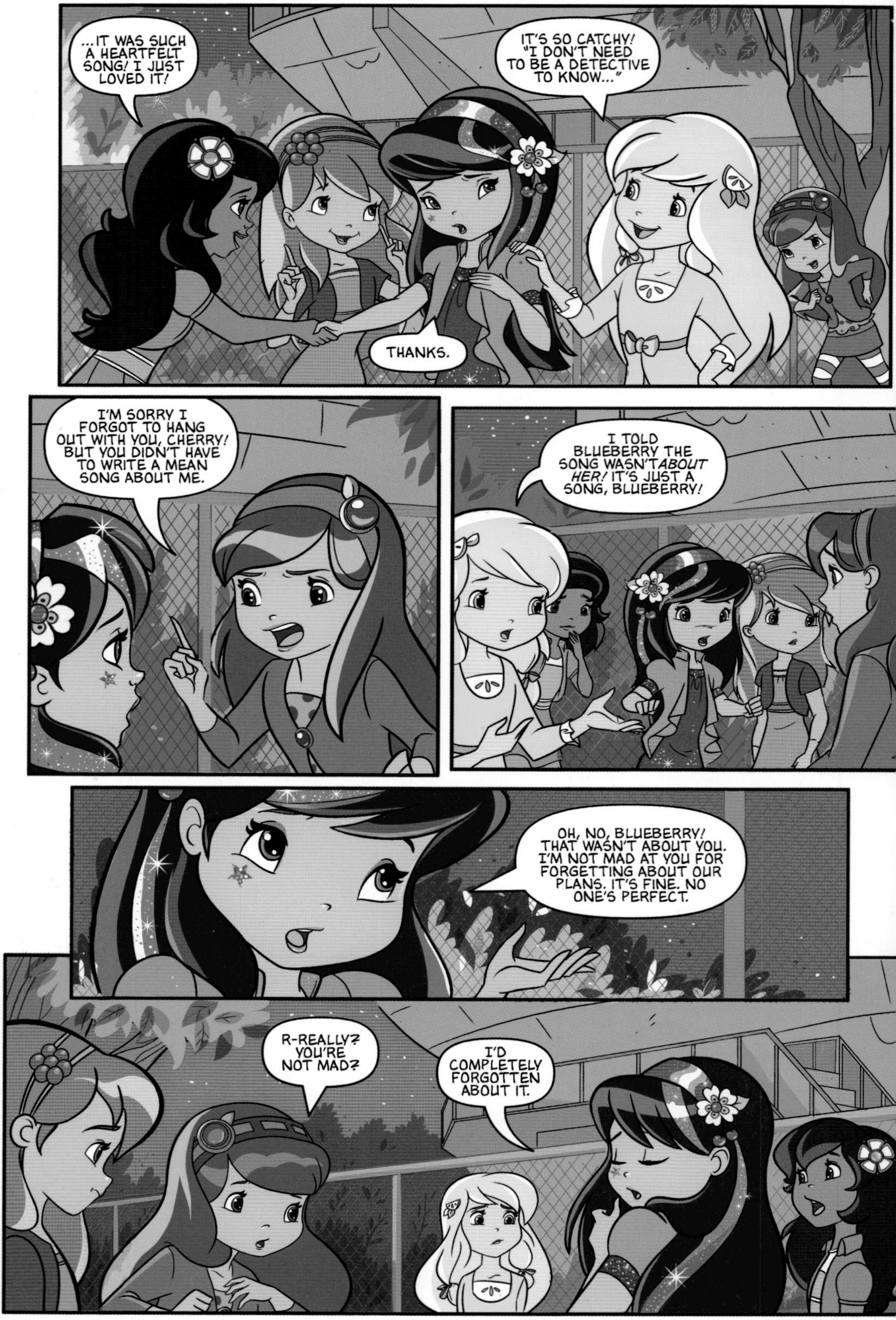
...IT WAS SUCH A HEARTFELT SONG! I JUST LOVED IT!
IT'S SO CATCHY! "I DON'T NEED TO BE A DETECTIVE TO KNOW..."
THANKS.
I'M SORRY I FORGOT TO HANG OUT WITH YOU, CHERRY! BUT YOU DIDN'T HAVE TO WRITE A MEAN SONG ABOUT ME.
I TOLD BLUEBERRY THE SONG WASN'T *ABOUT HER!* IT'S JUST A SONG, BLUEBERRY!
OH, NO, BLUEBERRY! THAT WASN'T ABOUT YOU. I'M NOT MAD AT YOU FOR FORGETTING ABOUT OUR PLANS. IT'S FINE. NO ONE'S PERFECT.
R-REALLY? YOU'RE NOT MAD?
I'D COMPLETELY FORGOTTEN ABOUT IT.

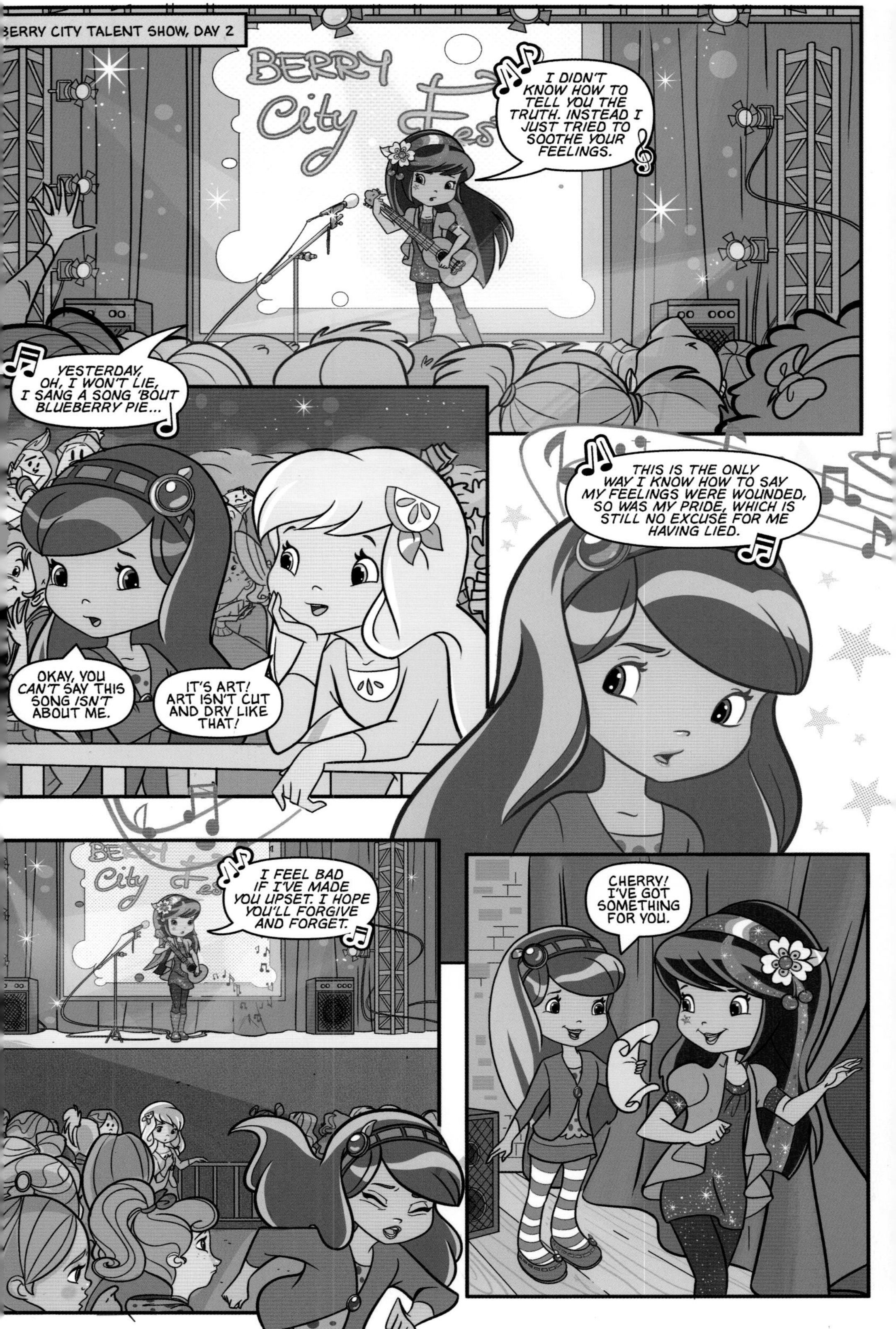
BERRY CITY TALENT SHOW, DAY 2
BERRY City Fest
I DIDN'T KNOW HOW TO TELL YOU THE TRUTH. INSTEAD I JUST TRIED TO SOOTHE YOUR FEELINGS.
YESTERDAY, OH, I WON'T LIE, I SANG A SONG 'BOUT BLUEBERRY PIE...
OKAY, YOU CAN'T SAY THIS SONG ISN'T ABOUT ME.
IT'S ART! ART ISN'T CUT AND DRY LIKE THAT!
THIS IS THE ONLY WAY I KNOW HOW TO SAY MY FEELINGS WERE WOUNDED, SO WAS MY PRIDE, WHICH IS STILL NO EXCUSE FOR ME HAVING LIED.
I FEEL BAD IF I'VE MADE YOU UPSET. I HOPE YOU'LL FORGIVE AND FORGET.
CHERRY! I'VE GOT SOMETHING FOR YOU.

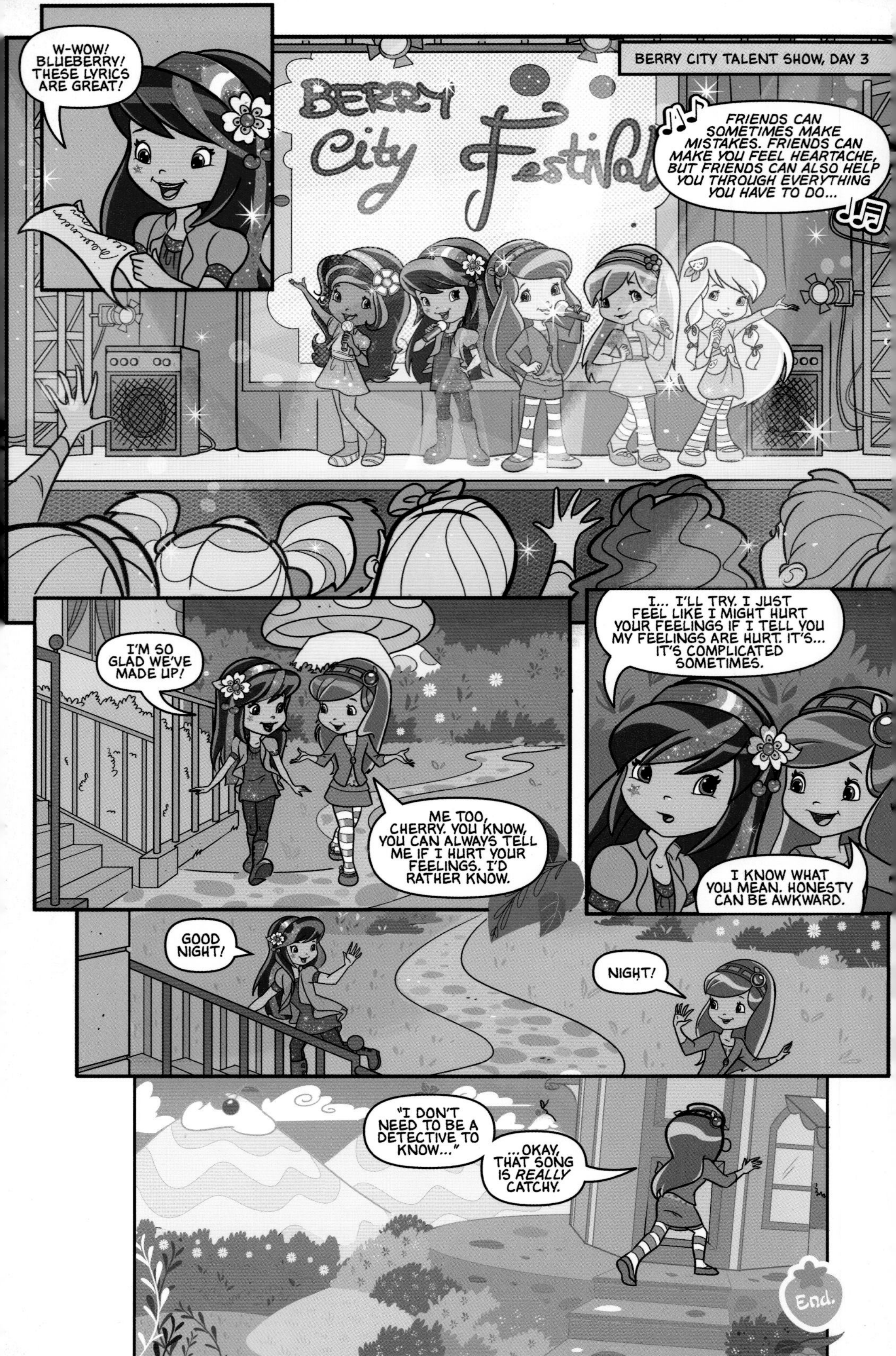
W-WOW! BLUEBERRY! THESE LYRICS ARE GREAT!
BERRY CITY TALENT SHOW, DAY 3
BERRY City Festival
FRIENDS CAN SOMETIMES MAKE MISTAKES. FRIENDS CAN MAKE YOU FEEL HEARTACHE, BUT FRIENDS CAN ALSO HELP YOU THROUGH EVERYTHING YOU HAVE TO DO...
I'M SO GLAD WE'VE MADE UP!
ME TOO, CHERRY. YOU KNOW, YOU CAN ALWAYS TELL ME IF I HURT YOUR FEELINGS. I'D RATHER KNOW.
I... I'LL TRY. I JUST FEEL LIKE I MIGHT HURT YOUR FEELINGS IF I TELL YOU MY FEELINGS ARE HURT. IT'S... IT'S COMPLICATED SOMETIMES.
I KNOW WHAT YOU MEAN. HONESTY CAN BE AWKWARD.
GOOD NIGHT!
NIGHT!
"I DON'T NEED TO BE A DETECTIVE TO KNOW..."
...OKAY, THAT SONG IS *REALLY* CATCHY.
End.

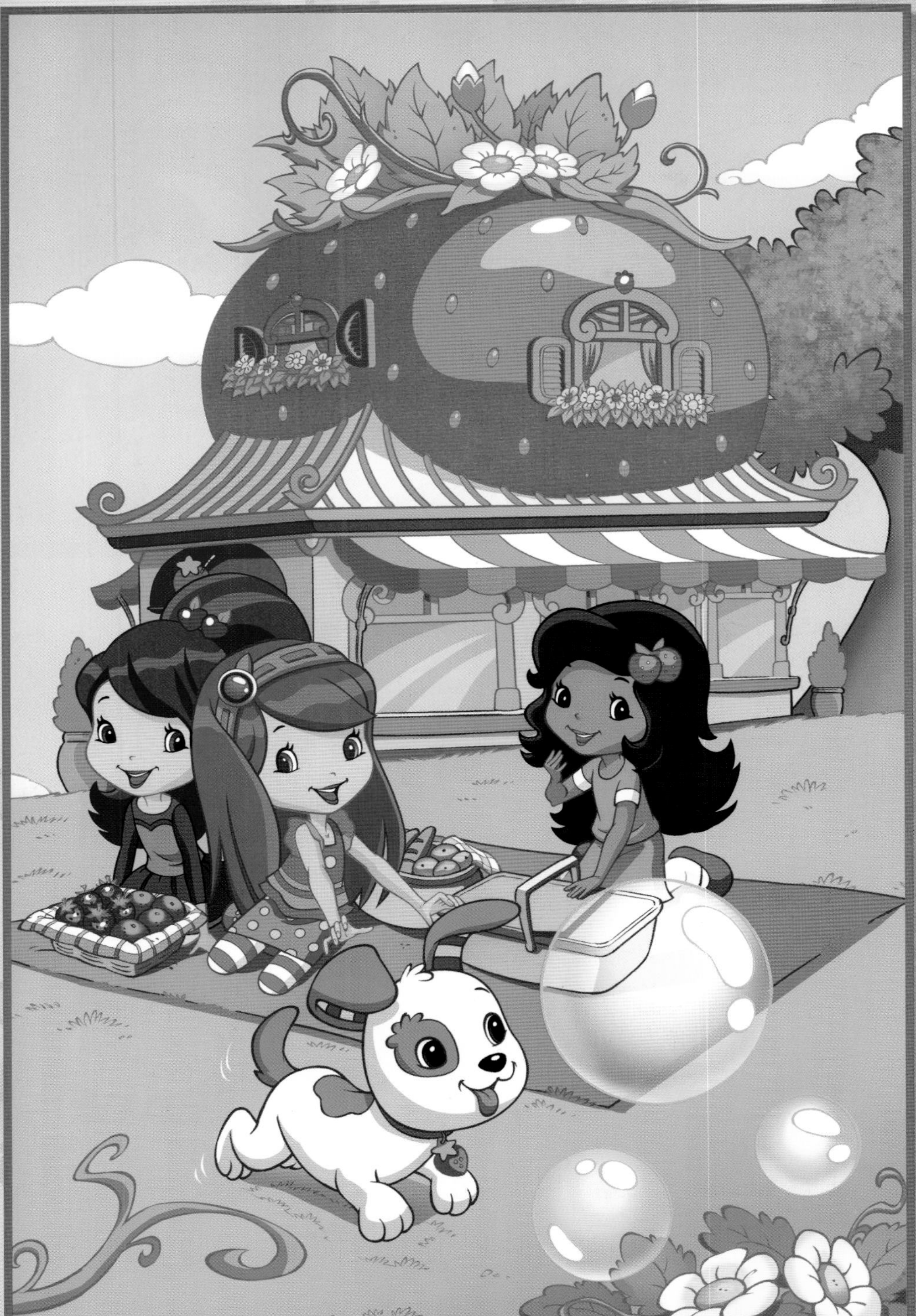

COVER ART BY Tina Franscisco

COVER COLORS BY Mae Hao

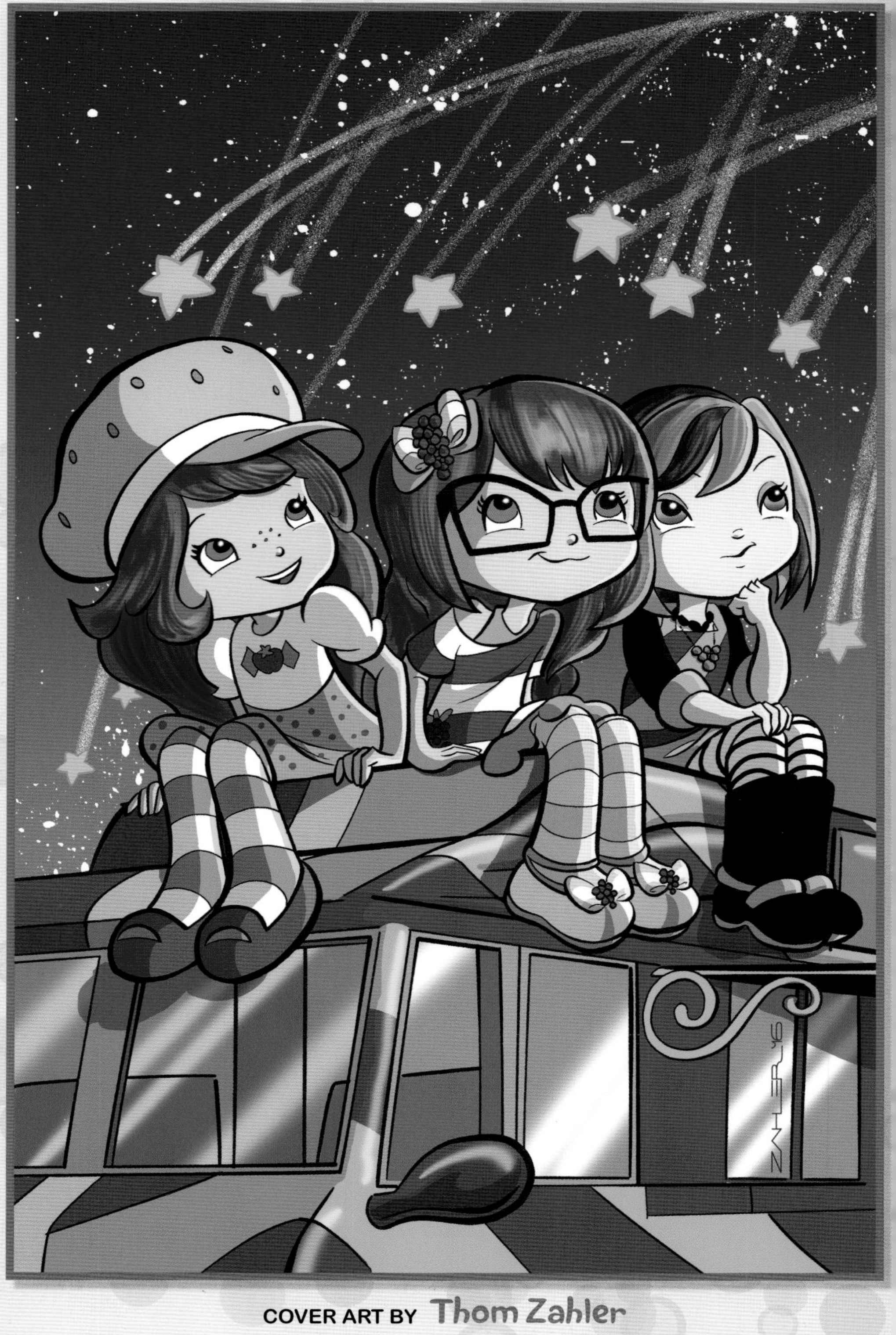
ZAHLER '16

COVER ART BY **Thom Zahler**

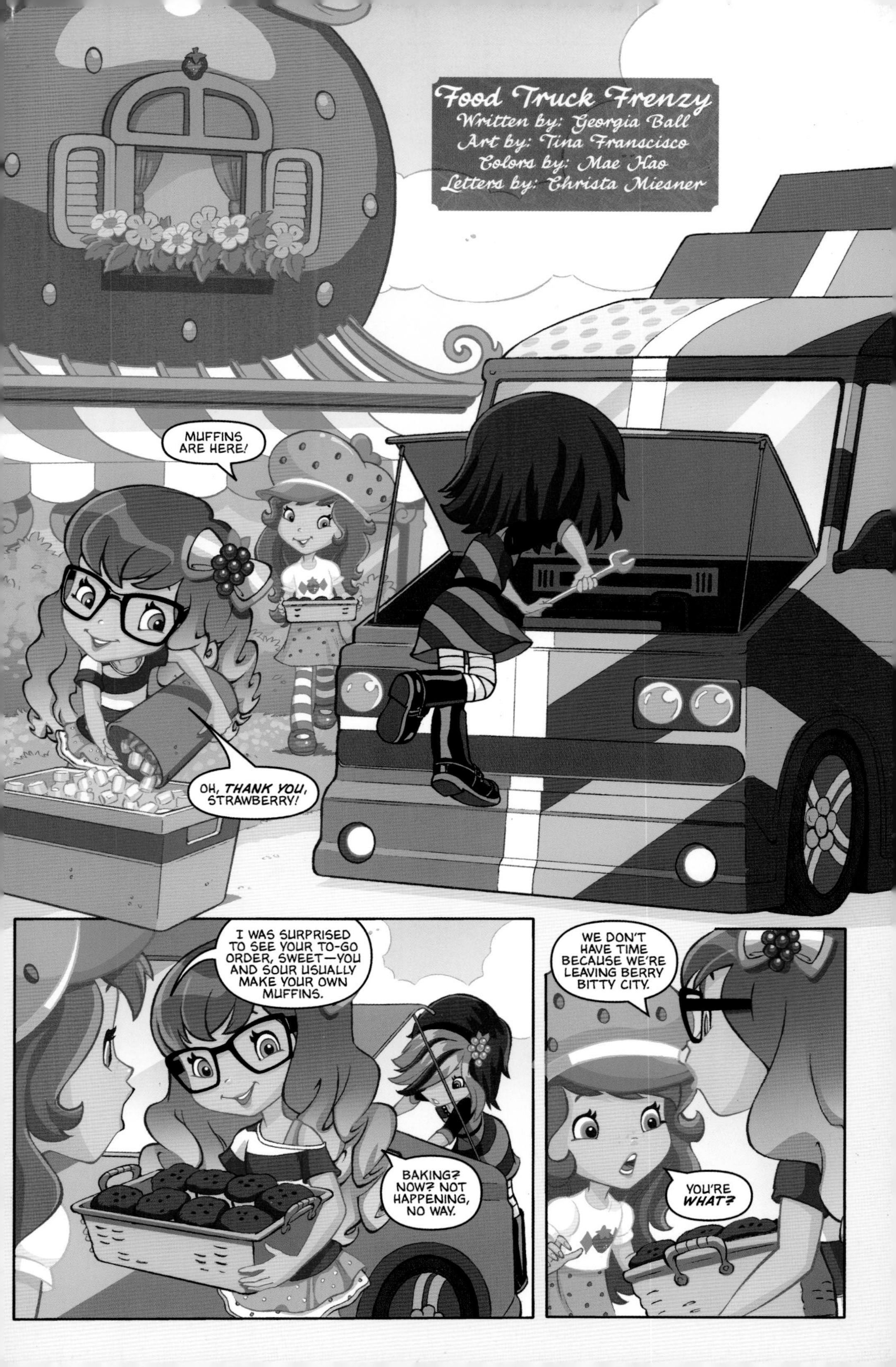
Food Truck Frenzy
Written by: Georgia Ball
Art by: Tina Franscisco
Colors by: Mae Hao
Letters by: Christa Miesner
MUFFINS ARE HERE!
OH, *THANK YOU*, STRAWBERRY!
I WAS SURPRISED TO SEE YOUR TO-GO ORDER, SWEET—YOU AND SOUR USUALLY MAKE YOUR OWN MUFFINS.
BAKING? NOW? NOT HAPPENING, NO WAY.
WE DON'T HAVE TIME BECAUSE WE'RE LEAVING BERRY BITTY CITY.
YOU'RE *WHAT?*

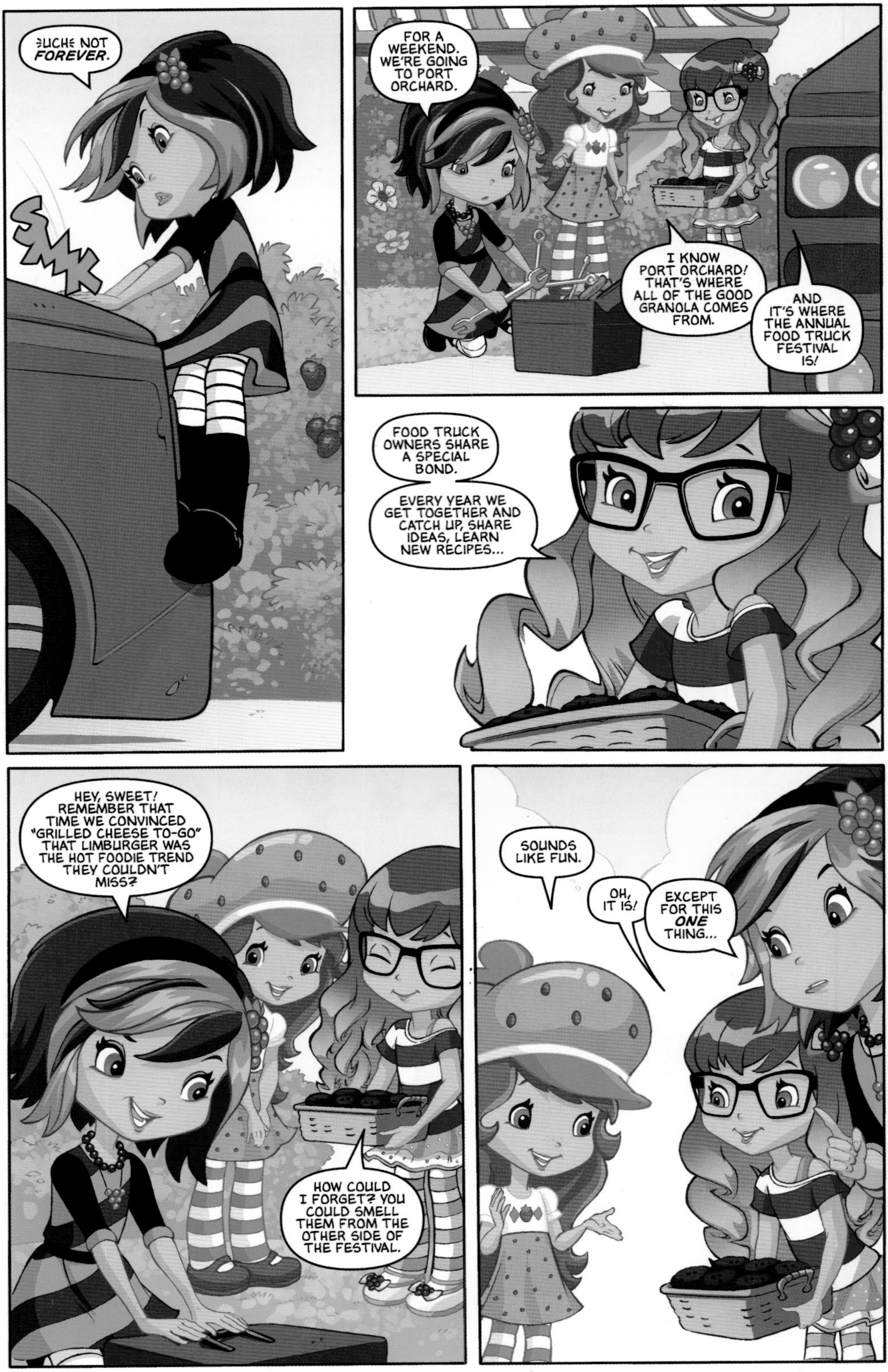
UCH NOT *FOREVER*.
SMAK
FOR A WEEKEND. WE'RE GOING TO PORT ORCHARD.
I KNOW PORT ORCHARD! THAT'S WHERE ALL OF THE GOOD GRANOLA COMES FROM.
AND IT'S WHERE THE ANNUAL FOOD TRUCK FESTIVAL IS!
FOOD TRUCK OWNERS SHARE A SPECIAL BOND.
EVERY YEAR WE GET TOGETHER AND CATCH UP, SHARE IDEAS, LEARN NEW RECIPES...
HEY, SWEET! REMEMBER THAT TIME WE CONVINCED "GRILLED CHEESE TO-GO" THAT LIMBURGER WAS THE HOT FOODIE TREND THEY COULDN'T MISS?
HOW COULD I FORGET? YOU COULD SMELL THEM FROM THE OTHER SIDE OF THE FESTIVAL.
SOUNDS LIKE FUN.
OH, IT IS!
EXCEPT FOR THIS *ONE* THING...

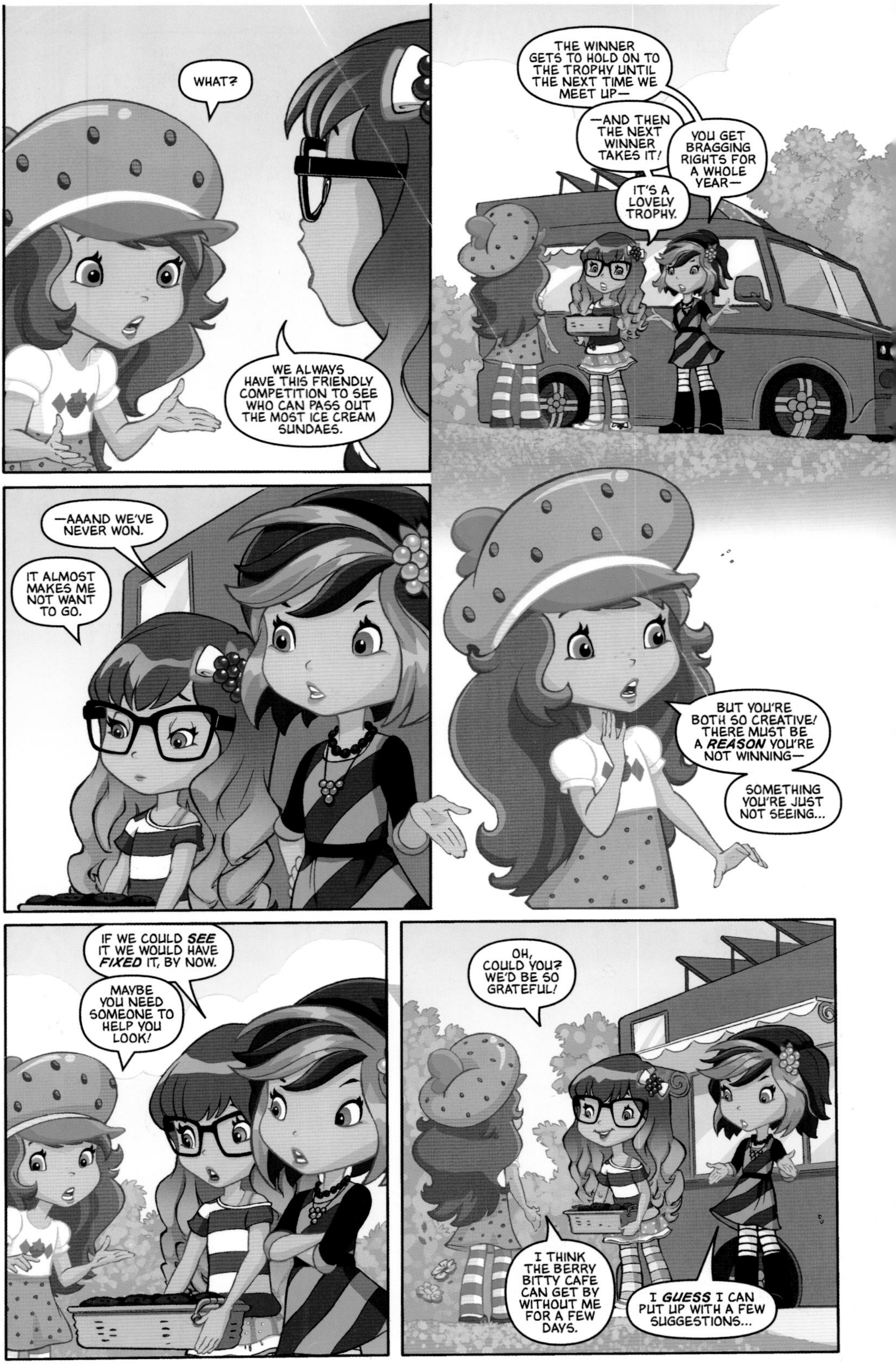
WHAT?
WE ALWAYS HAVE THIS FRIENDLY COMPETITION TO SEE WHO CAN PASS OUT THE MOST ICE CREAM SUNDAES.
THE WINNER GETS TO HOLD ON TO THE TROPHY UNTIL THE NEXT TIME WE MEET UP—
—AND THEN THE NEXT WINNER TAKES IT!
YOU GET BRAGGING RIGHTS FOR A WHOLE YEAR—
IT'S A LOVELY TROPHY.
—AAAND WE'VE NEVER WON.
IT ALMOST MAKES ME NOT WANT TO GO.
BUT YOU'RE BOTH SO CREATIVE! THERE MUST BE A REASON YOU'RE NOT WINNING—
SOMETHING YOU'RE JUST NOT SEEING...
IF WE COULD SEE IT WE WOULD HAVE FIXED IT, BY NOW.
MAYBE YOU NEED SOMEONE TO HELP YOU LOOK!
OH, COULD YOU? WE'D BE SO GRATEFUL!
I THINK THE BERRY BITTY CAFE CAN GET BY WITHOUT ME FOR A FEW DAYS.
I GUESS I CAN PUT UP WITH A FEW SUGGESTIONS...

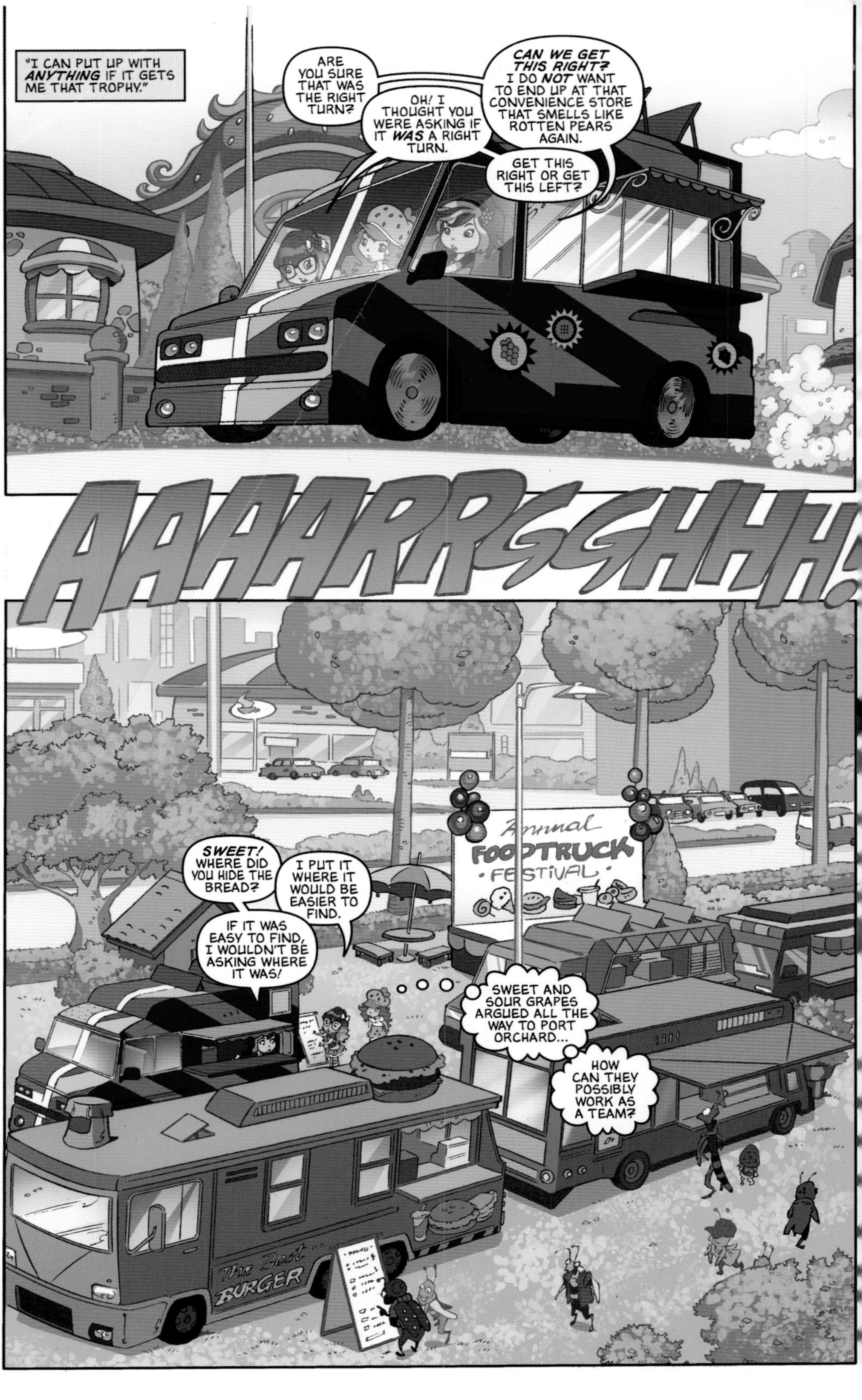

"I CAN PUT UP WITH ANYTHING IF IT GETS ME THAT TROPHY."
ARE YOU SURE THAT WAS THE RIGHT TURN?
OH! I THOUGHT YOU WERE ASKING IF IT WAS A RIGHT TURN.
CAN WE GET THIS RIGHT? I DO NOT WANT TO END UP AT THAT CONVENIENCE STORE THAT SMELLS LIKE ROTTEN PEARS AGAIN.
GET THIS RIGHT OR GET THIS LEFT?
AAAARRGGHHH!
Annual FOODTRUCK FESTIVAL
SWEET! WHERE DID YOU HIDE THE BREAD?
I PUT IT WHERE IT WOULD BE EASIER TO FIND.
IF IT WAS EASY TO FIND, I WOULDN'T BE ASKING WHERE IT WAS!
SWEET AND SOUR GRAPES ARGUED ALL THE WAY TO PORT ORCHARD...
HOW CAN THEY POSSIBLY WORK AS A TEAM?
The Best BURGER

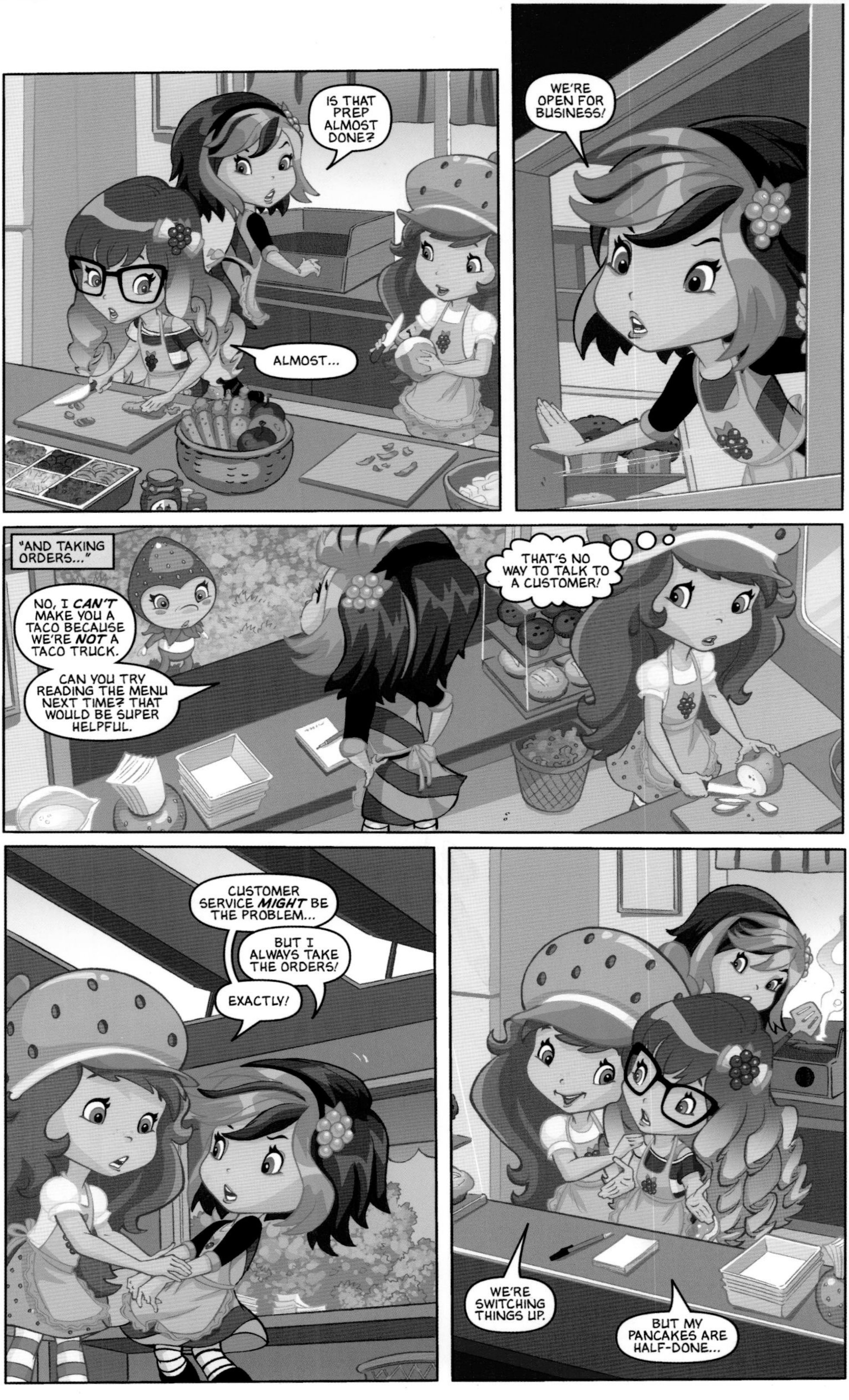
IS THAT PREP ALMOST DONE?
ALMOST...
WE'RE OPEN FOR BUSINESS!
"AND TAKING ORDERS..."
NO, I CAN'T MAKE YOU A TACO BECAUSE WE'RE NOT A TACO TRUCK.
CAN YOU TRY READING THE MENU NEXT TIME? THAT WOULD BE SUPER HELPFUL.
THAT'S NO WAY TO TALK TO A CUSTOMER!
CUSTOMER SERVICE MIGHT BE THE PROBLEM...
BUT I ALWAYS TAKE THE ORDERS!
EXACTLY!
WE'RE SWITCHING THINGS UP.
BUT MY PANCAKES ARE HALF-DONE...

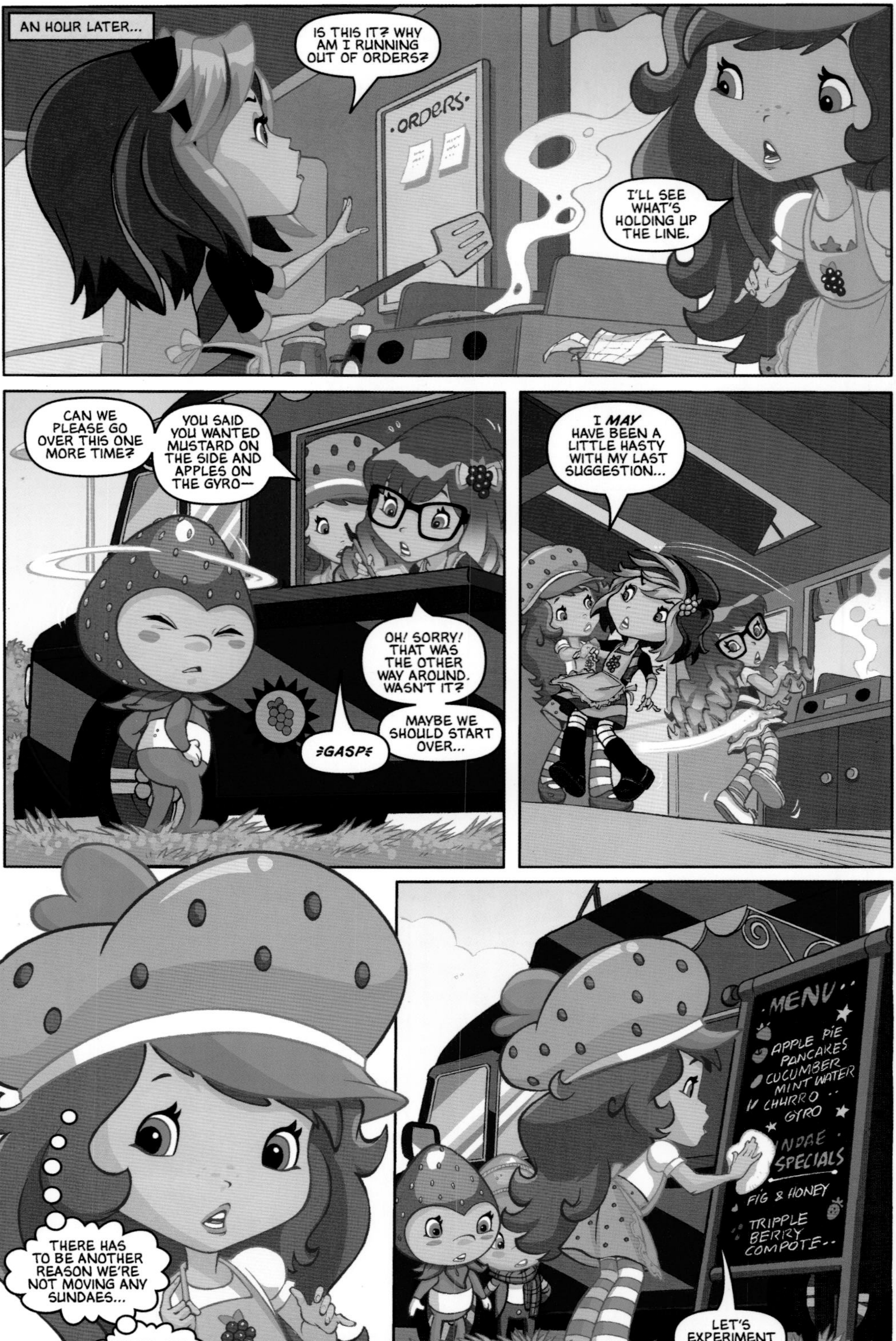
AN HOUR LATER...
IS THIS IT? WHY AM I RUNNING OUT OF ORDERS?
ORDERS
I'LL SEE WHAT'S HOLDING UP THE LINE.
CAN WE PLEASE GO OVER THIS ONE MORE TIME?
YOU SAID YOU WANTED MUSTARD ON THE SIDE AND APPLES ON THE GYRO—
OH! SORRY! THAT WAS THE OTHER WAY AROUND. WASN'T IT?
GASP
MAYBE WE SHOULD START OVER...
I *MAY* HAVE BEEN A LITTLE HASTY WITH MY LAST SUGGESTION...
THERE HAS TO BE ANOTHER REASON WE'RE NOT MOVING ANY SUNDAES...
MAYBE IT'S THE MENU?
MENU
APPLE PIE PANCAKES
CUCUMBER MINT WATER
CHURRO
GYRO
NDAE SPECIALS
FIG & HONEY
TRIPPLE BERRY COMPOTE
LET'S EXPERIMENT A LITTLE...

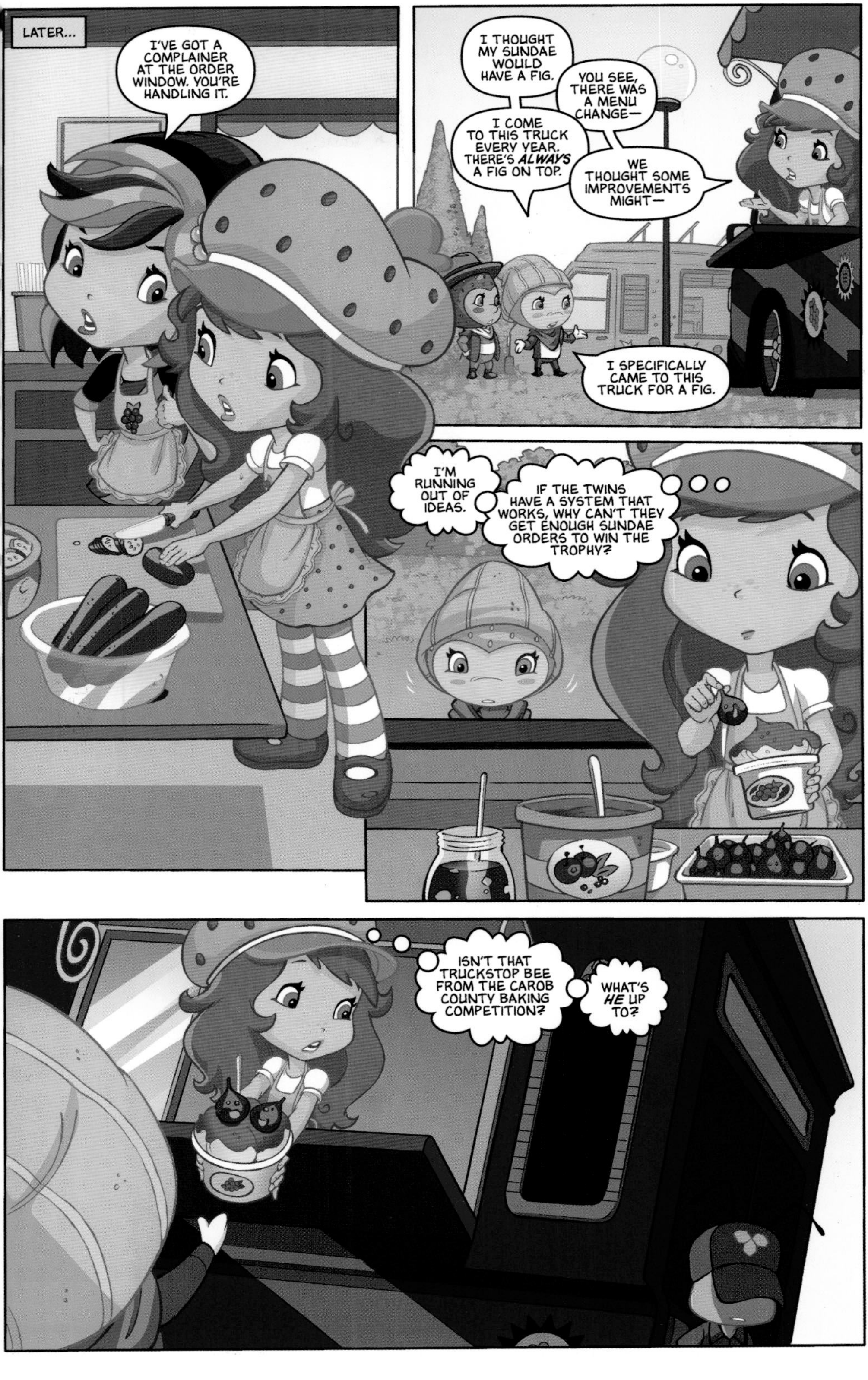
LATER...
I'VE GOT A COMPLAINER AT THE ORDER WINDOW. YOU'RE HANDLING IT.
I THOUGHT MY SUNDAE WOULD HAVE A FIG.
I COME TO THIS TRUCK EVERY YEAR. THERE'S ALWAYS A FIG ON TOP.
YOU SEE, THERE WAS A MENU CHANGE—
WE THOUGHT SOME IMPROVEMENTS MIGHT—
I SPECIFICALLY CAME TO THIS TRUCK FOR A FIG.
I'M RUNNING OUT OF IDEAS.
IF THE TWINS HAVE A SYSTEM THAT WORKS, WHY CAN'T THEY GET ENOUGH SUNDAE ORDERS TO WIN THE TROPHY?
ISN'T THAT TRUCKSTOP BEE FROM THE CAROB COUNTY BAKING COMPETITION?
WHAT'S HE UP TO?

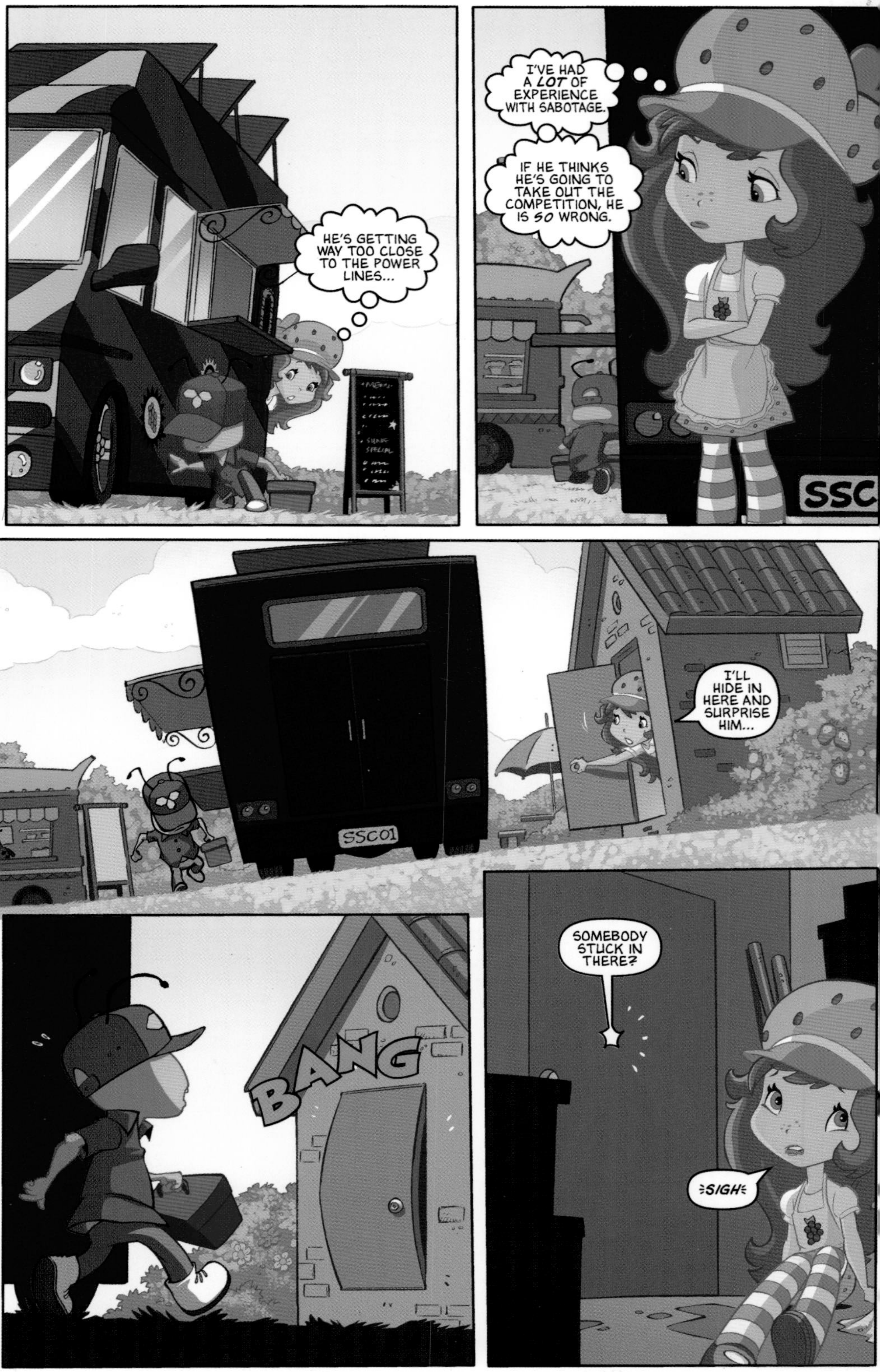
HE'S GETTING WAY TOO CLOSE TO THE POWER LINES...
I'VE HAD A LOT OF EXPERIENCE WITH SABOTAGE.
IF HE THINKS HE'S GOING TO TAKE OUT THE COMPETITION, HE IS SO WRONG.
SSC
SSC01
I'LL HIDE IN HERE AND SURPRISE HIM...
BANG
SOMEBODY STUCK IN THERE?
SIGH

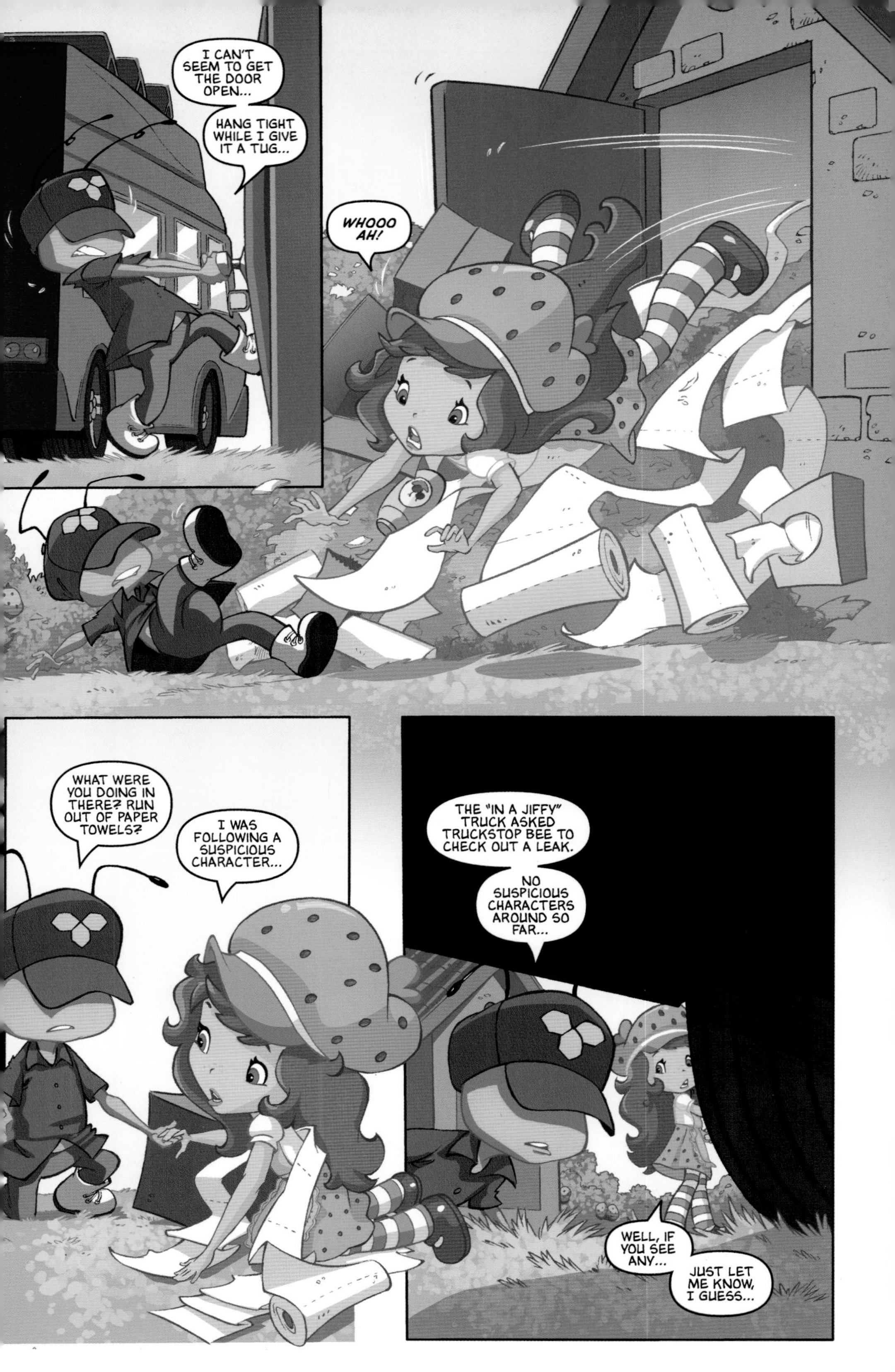
I CAN'T SEEM TO GET THE DOOR OPEN...
HANG TIGHT WHILE I GIVE IT A TUG...
WHOOO AH!
WHAT WERE YOU DOING IN THERE? RUN OUT OF PAPER TOWELS?
I WAS FOLLOWING A SUSPICIOUS CHARACTER...
THE "IN A JIFFY" TRUCK ASKED TRUCKSTOP BEE TO CHECK OUT A LEAK.
NO SUSPICIOUS CHARACTERS AROUND SO FAR...
WELL, IF YOU SEE ANY...
JUST LET ME KNOW, I GUESS...

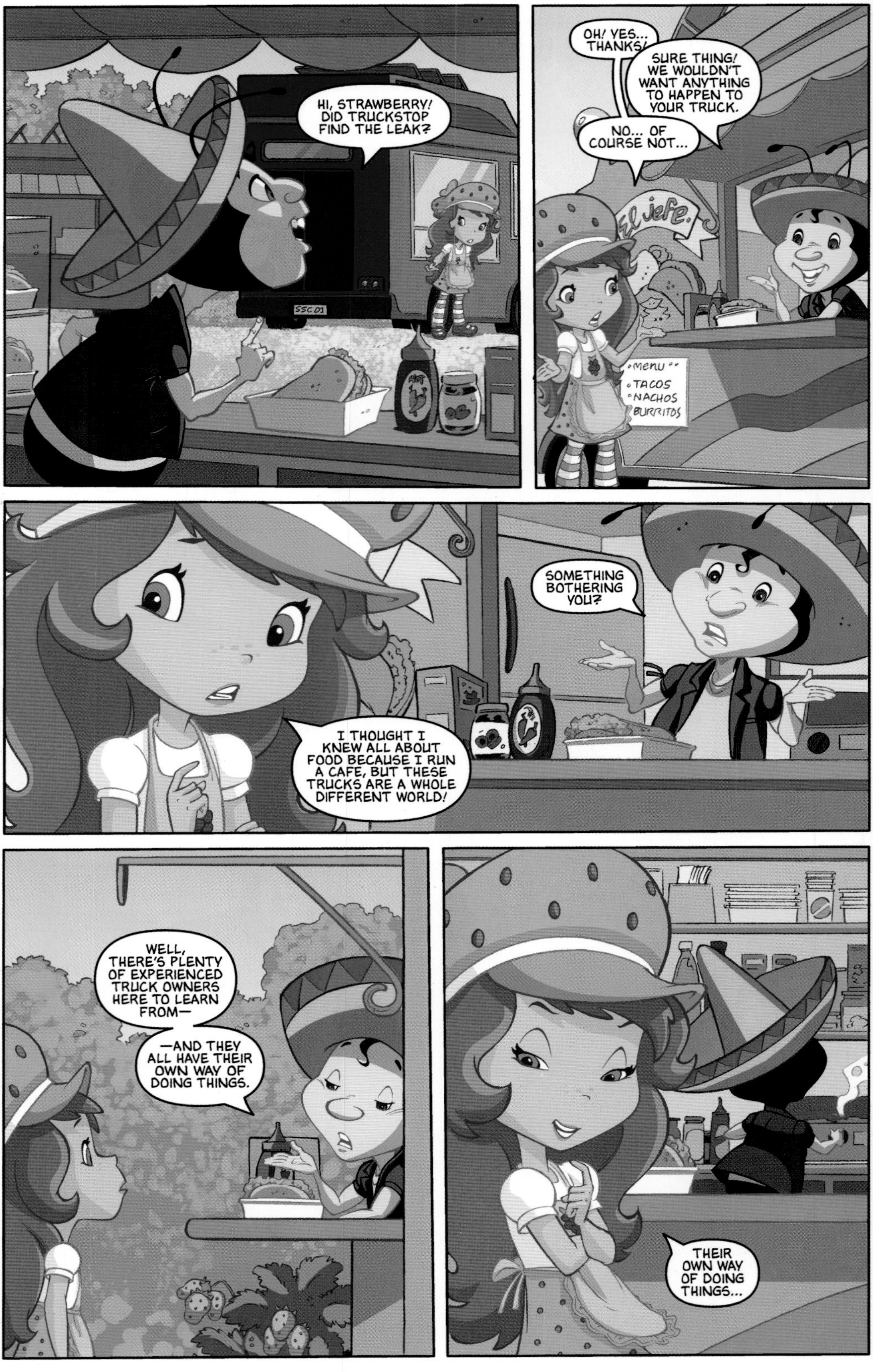
HI, STRAWBERRY! DID TRUCKSTOP FIND THE LEAK?
OH! YES... THANKS!
SURE THING! WE WOULDN'T WANT ANYTHING TO HAPPEN TO YOUR TRUCK.
NO... OF COURSE NOT...
El Jefe
Menu
TACOS
NACHOS
BURRITOS
SOMETHING BOTHERING YOU?
I THOUGHT I KNEW ALL ABOUT FOOD BECAUSE I RUN A CAFE, BUT THESE TRUCKS ARE A WHOLE DIFFERENT WORLD!
WELL, THERE'S PLENTY OF EXPERIENCED TRUCK OWNERS HERE TO LEARN FROM—
—AND THEY ALL HAVE THEIR OWN WAY OF DOING THINGS.
THEIR OWN WAY OF DOING THINGS...

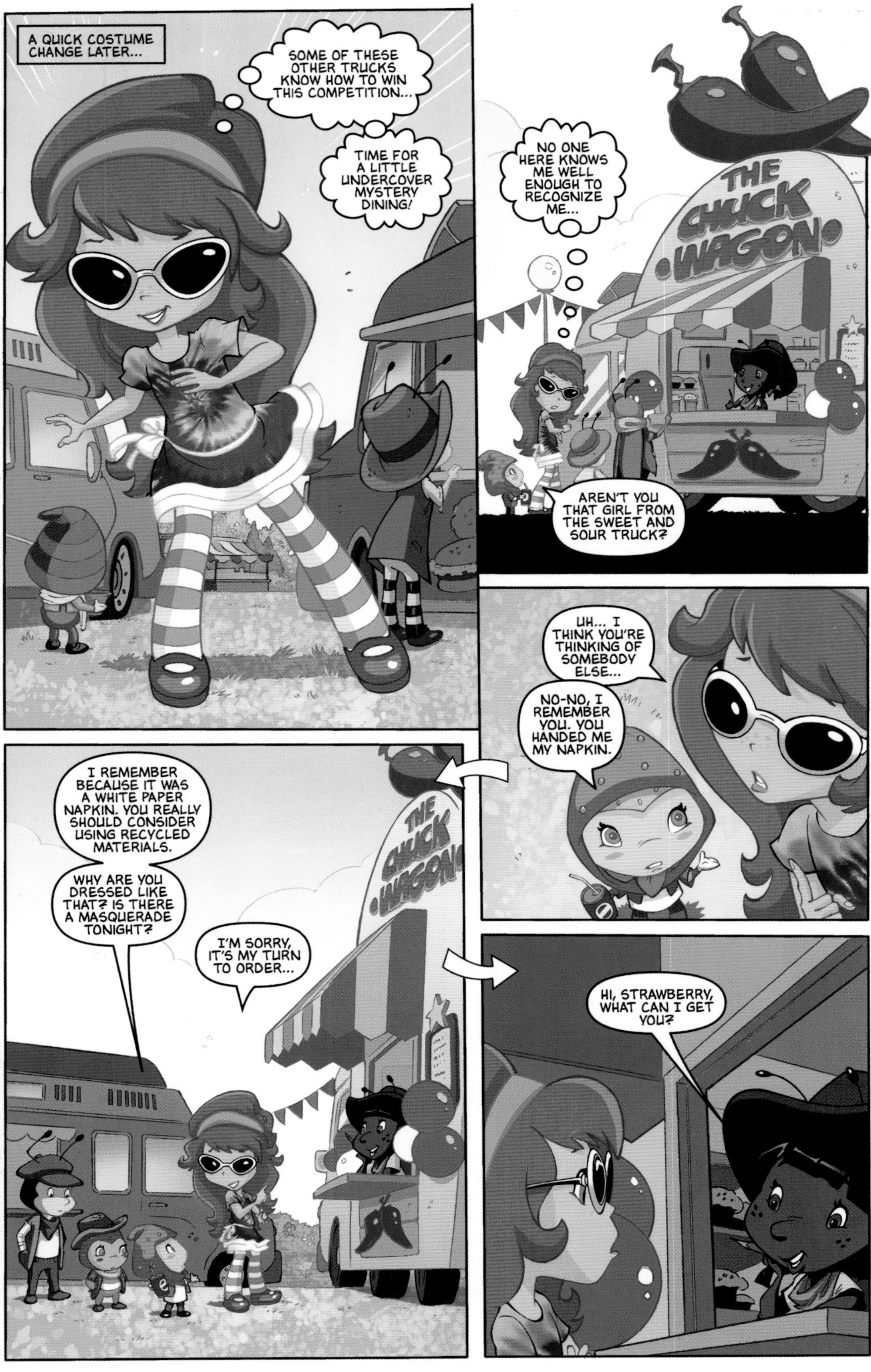
A QUICK COSTUME CHANGE LATER...
SOME OF THESE OTHER TRUCKS KNOW HOW TO WIN THIS COMPETITION...
TIME FOR A LITTLE UNDERCOVER MYSTERY DINING!
THE CHUCK WAGON
NO ONE HERE KNOWS ME WELL ENOUGH TO RECOGNIZE ME...
AREN'T YOU THAT GIRL FROM THE SWEET AND SOUR TRUCK?
UH... I THINK YOU'RE THINKING OF SOMEBODY ELSE...
NO-NO, I REMEMBER YOU. YOU HANDED ME MY NAPKIN.
I REMEMBER BECAUSE IT WAS A WHITE PAPER NAPKIN. YOU REALLY SHOULD CONSIDER USING RECYCLED MATERIALS.
WHY ARE YOU DRESSED LIKE THAT? IS THERE A MASQUERADE TONIGHT?
THE CHUCK WAGON
I'M SORRY, IT'S MY TURN TO ORDER...
HI, STRAWBERRY, WHAT CAN I GET YOU?

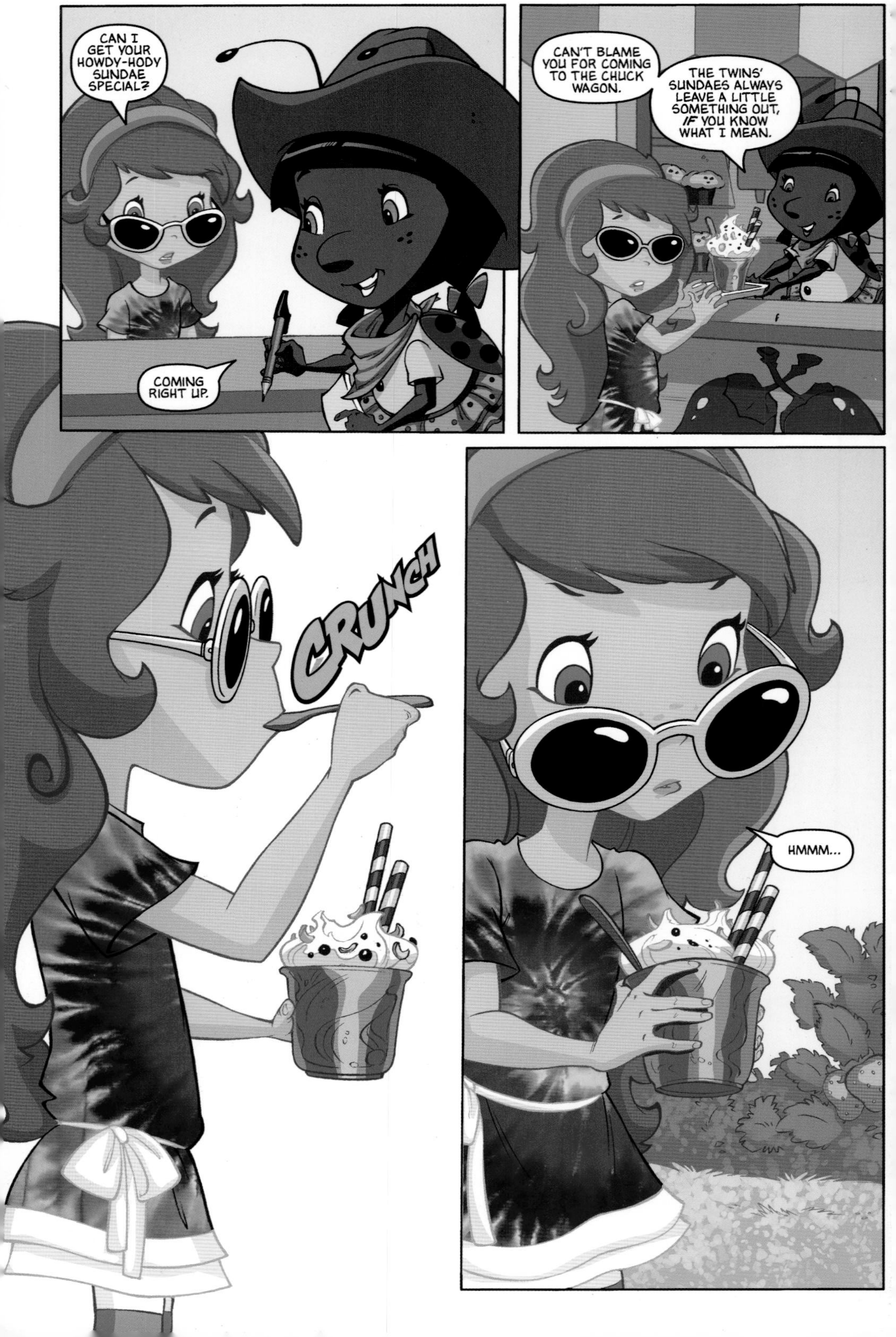
CAN I GET YOUR HOWDY-HODY SUNDAE SPECIAL?
COMING RIGHT UP.
CAN'T BLAME YOU FOR COMING TO THE CHUCK WAGON.
THE TWINS' SUNDAES ALWAYS LEAVE A LITTLE SOMETHING OUT, *IF* YOU KNOW WHAT I MEAN.
CRUNCH
HMMM...

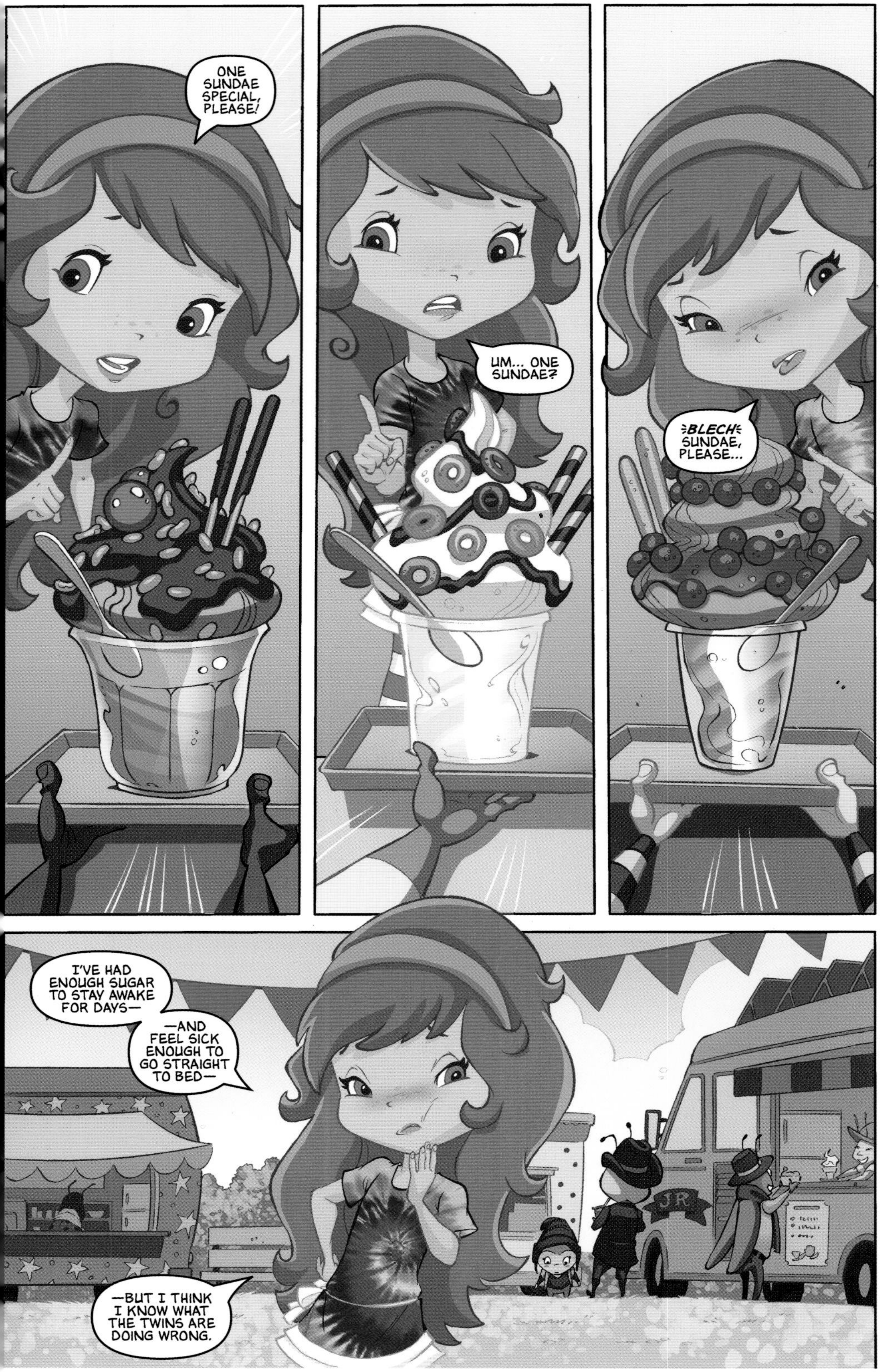
ONE SUNDAE SPECIAL, PLEASE!
UM... ONE SUNDAE?
BLECH SUNDAE, PLEASE...
I'VE HAD ENOUGH SUGAR TO STAY AWAKE FOR DAYS—
—AND FEEL SICK ENOUGH TO GO STRAIGHT TO BED—
—BUT I THINK I KNOW WHAT THE TWINS ARE DOING WRONG.
J.R.

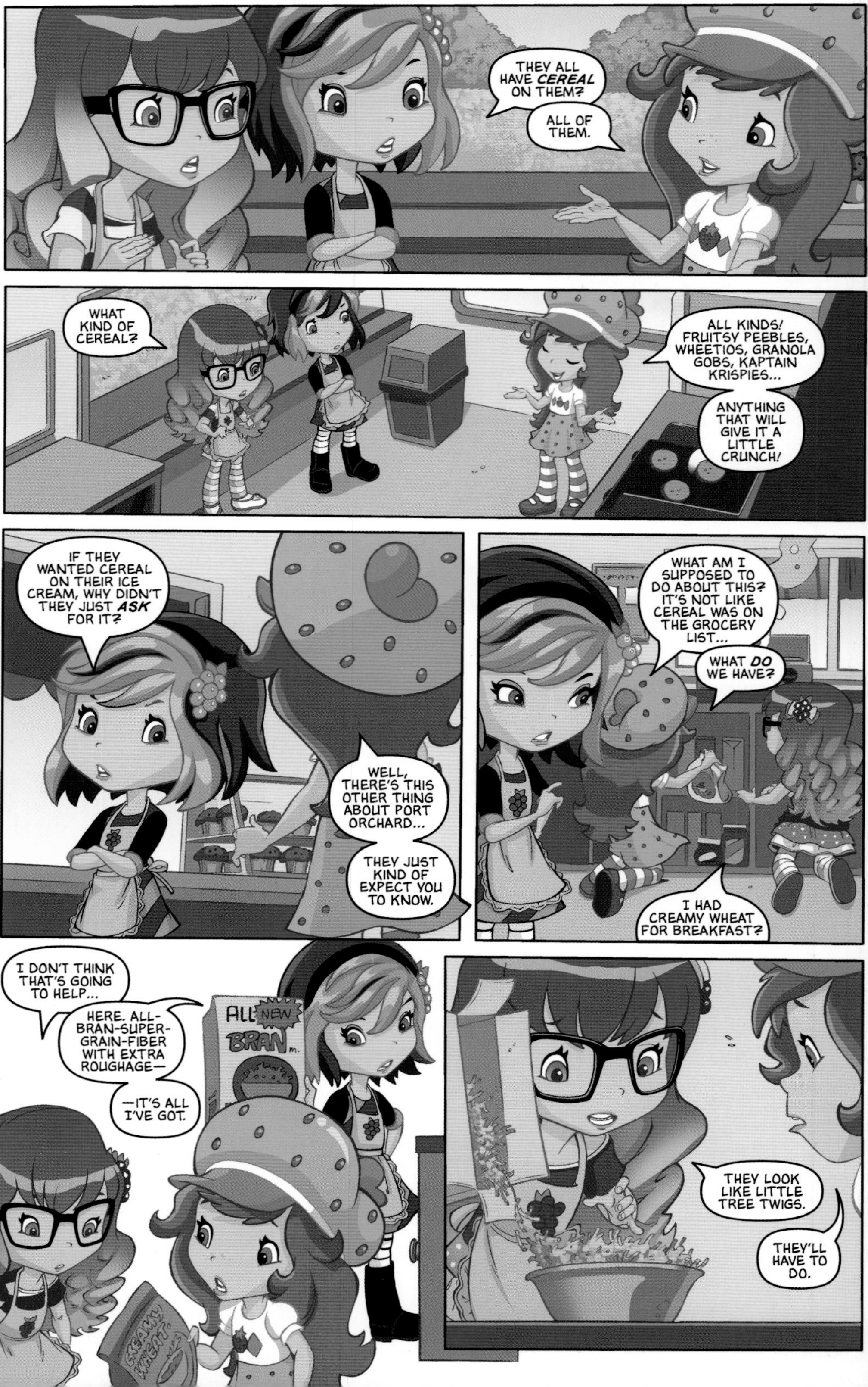
THEY ALL HAVE *CEREAL* ON THEM?
ALL OF THEM.
WHAT KIND OF CEREAL?
ALL KINDS! FRUITSY PEEBLES, WHEETIOS, GRANOLA GOBS, KAPTAIN KRISPIES...
ANYTHING THAT WILL GIVE IT A LITTLE CRUNCH!
IF THEY WANTED CEREAL ON THEIR ICE CREAM, WHY DIDN'T THEY JUST *ASK* FOR IT?
WELL, THERE'S THIS OTHER THING ABOUT PORT ORCHARD...
THEY JUST KIND OF EXPECT YOU TO KNOW.
WHAT AM I SUPPOSED TO DO ABOUT THIS? IT'S NOT LIKE CEREAL WAS ON THE GROCERY LIST...
WHAT *DO* WE HAVE?
I HAD CREAMY WHEAT FOR BREAKFAST?
I DON'T THINK THAT'S GOING TO HELP...
HERE. ALL-BRAN-SUPER-GRAIN-FIBER WITH EXTRA ROUGHAGE—
—IT'S ALL I'VE GOT.
ALL NEW BRAN
THEY LOOK LIKE LITTLE TREE TWIGS.
THEY'LL HAVE TO DO.

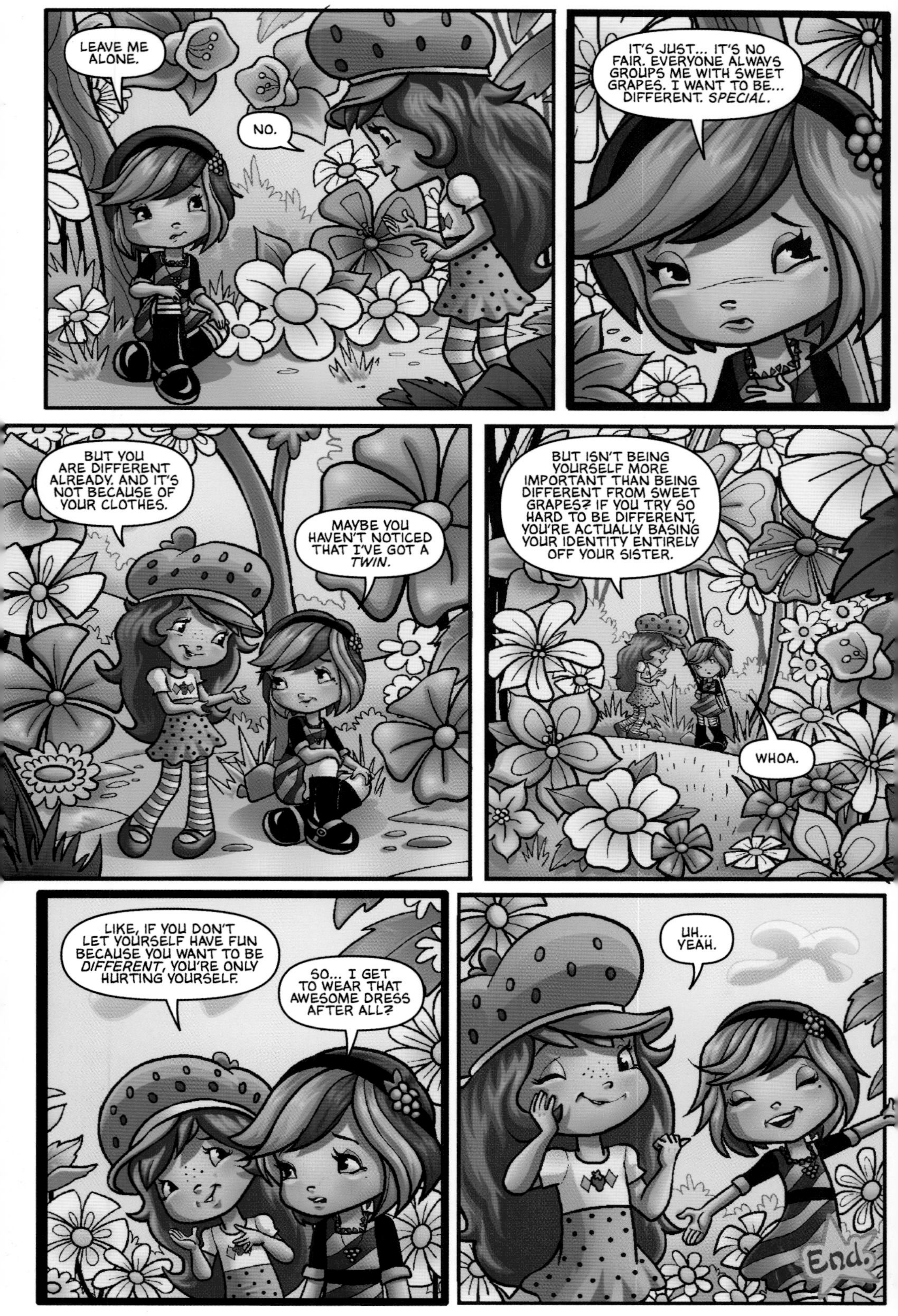
LEAVE ME ALONE.
NO.
IT'S JUST... IT'S NO FAIR. EVERYONE ALWAYS GROUPS ME WITH SWEET GRAPES. I WANT TO BE... DIFFERENT. *SPECIAL*.
BUT YOU ARE DIFFERENT ALREADY. AND IT'S NOT BECAUSE OF YOUR CLOTHES.
MAYBE YOU HAVEN'T NOTICED THAT I'VE GOT A *TWIN*.
BUT ISN'T BEING YOURSELF MORE IMPORTANT THAN BEING DIFFERENT FROM SWEET GRAPES? IF YOU TRY SO HARD TO BE DIFFERENT, YOU'RE ACTUALLY BASING YOUR IDENTITY ENTIRELY OFF YOUR SISTER.
WHOA.
LIKE, IF YOU DON'T LET YOURSELF HAVE FUN BECAUSE YOU WANT TO BE *DIFFERENT*, YOU'RE ONLY HURTING YOURSELF.
SO... I GET TO WEAR THAT AWESOME DRESS AFTER ALL?
UH... YEAH.
End.

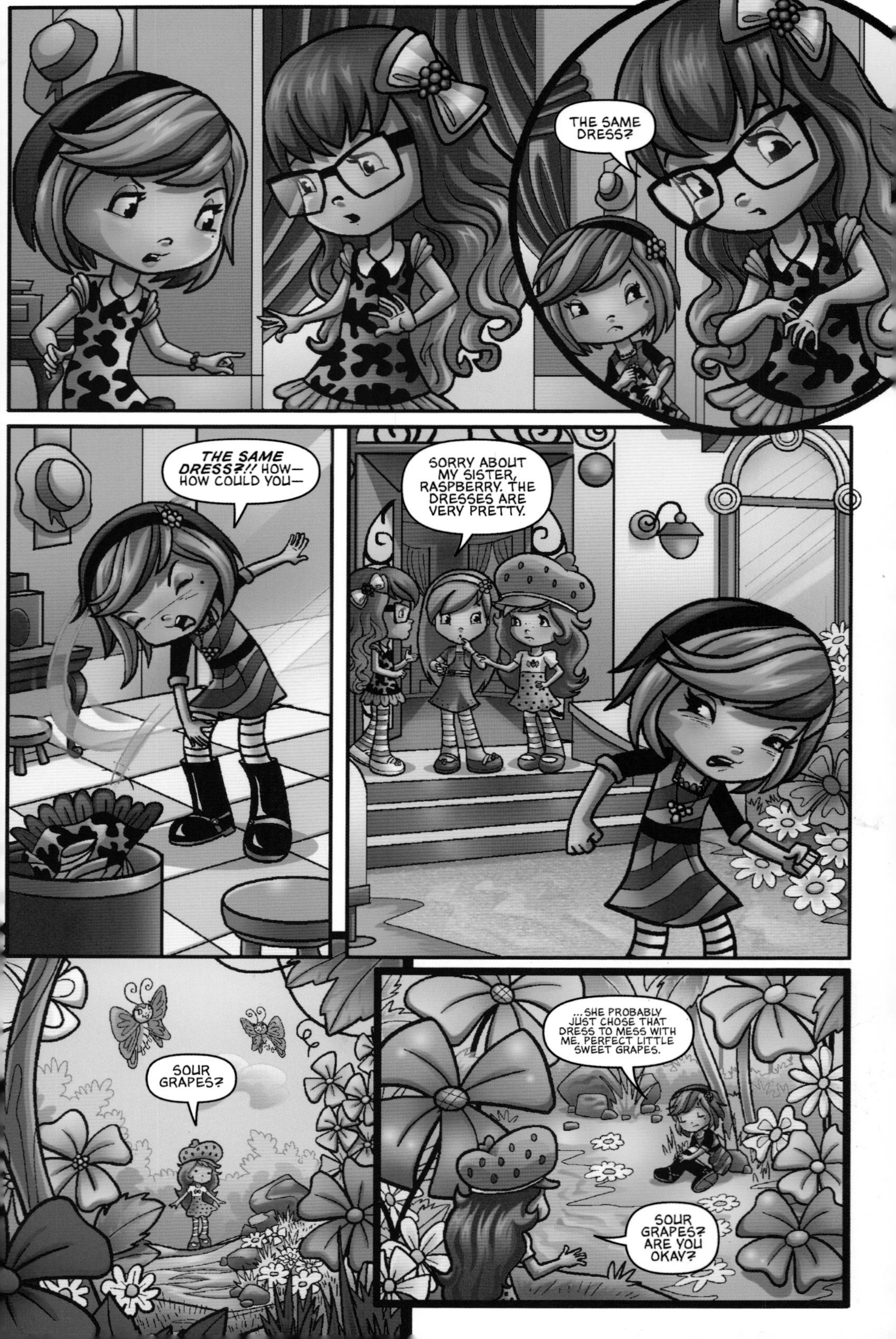
THE SAME DRESS?
THE SAME DRESS?!! HOW—HOW COULD YOU—
SORRY ABOUT MY SISTER, RASPBERRY. THE DRESSES ARE VERY PRETTY.
SOUR GRAPES?
...SHE PROBABLY JUST CHOSE THAT DRESS TO MESS WITH ME. PERFECT LITTLE SWEET GRAPES.
SOUR GRAPES? ARE YOU OKAY?

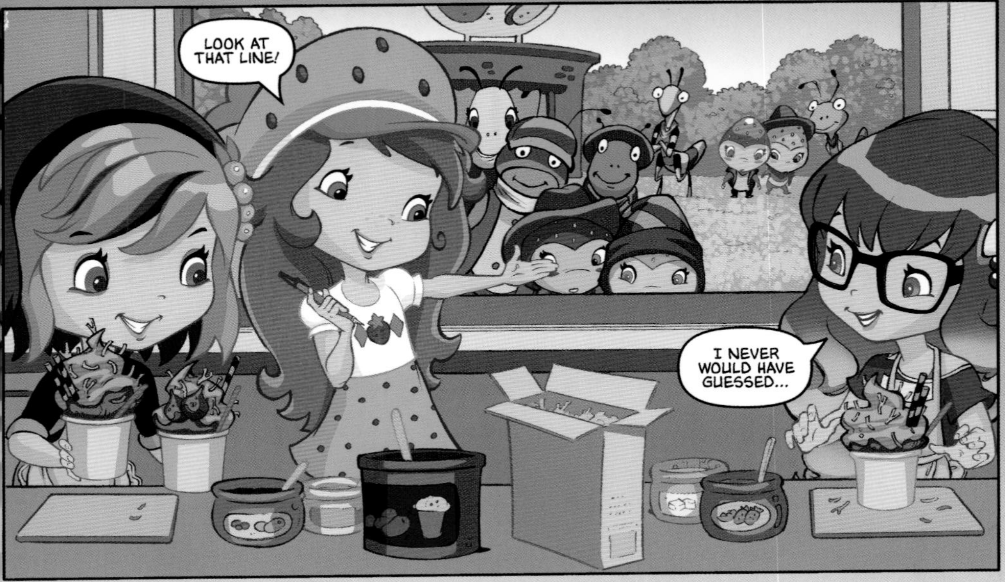
LOOK AT THAT LINE!
I NEVER WOULD HAVE GUESSED...

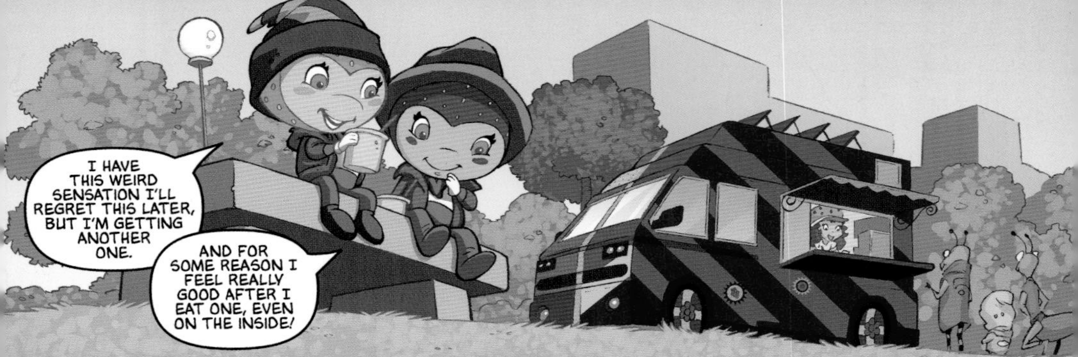
I HAVE THIS WEIRD SENSATION I'LL REGRET THIS LATER, BUT I'M GETTING ANOTHER ONE.
AND FOR SOME REASON I FEEL REALLY GOOD AFTER I EAT ONE, EVEN ON THE INSIDE!

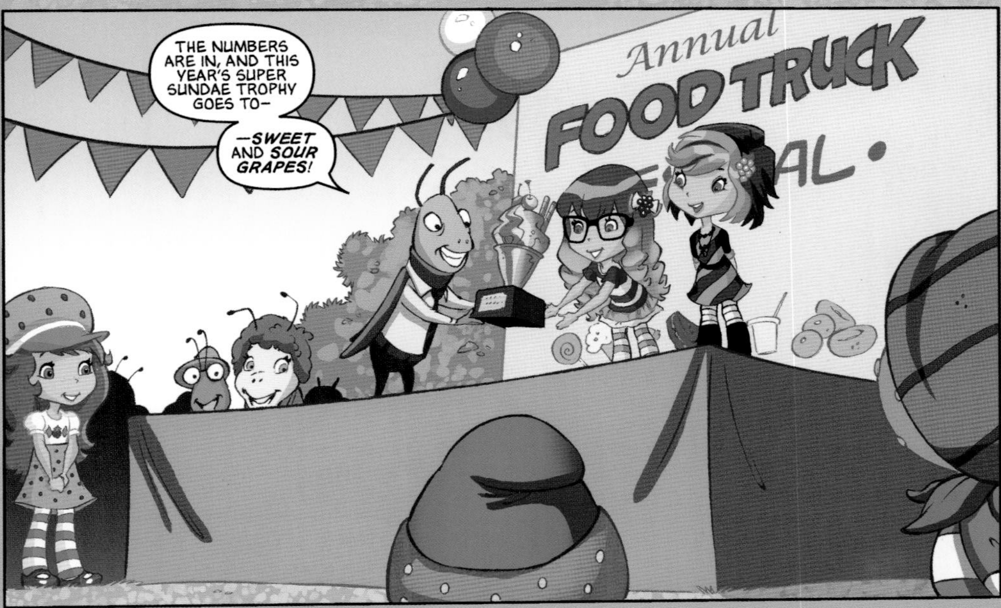
THE NUMBERS ARE IN, AND THIS YEAR'S SUPER SUNDAE TROPHY GOES TO—
—SWEET AND SOUR GRAPES!
Annual
FOOD TRUCK

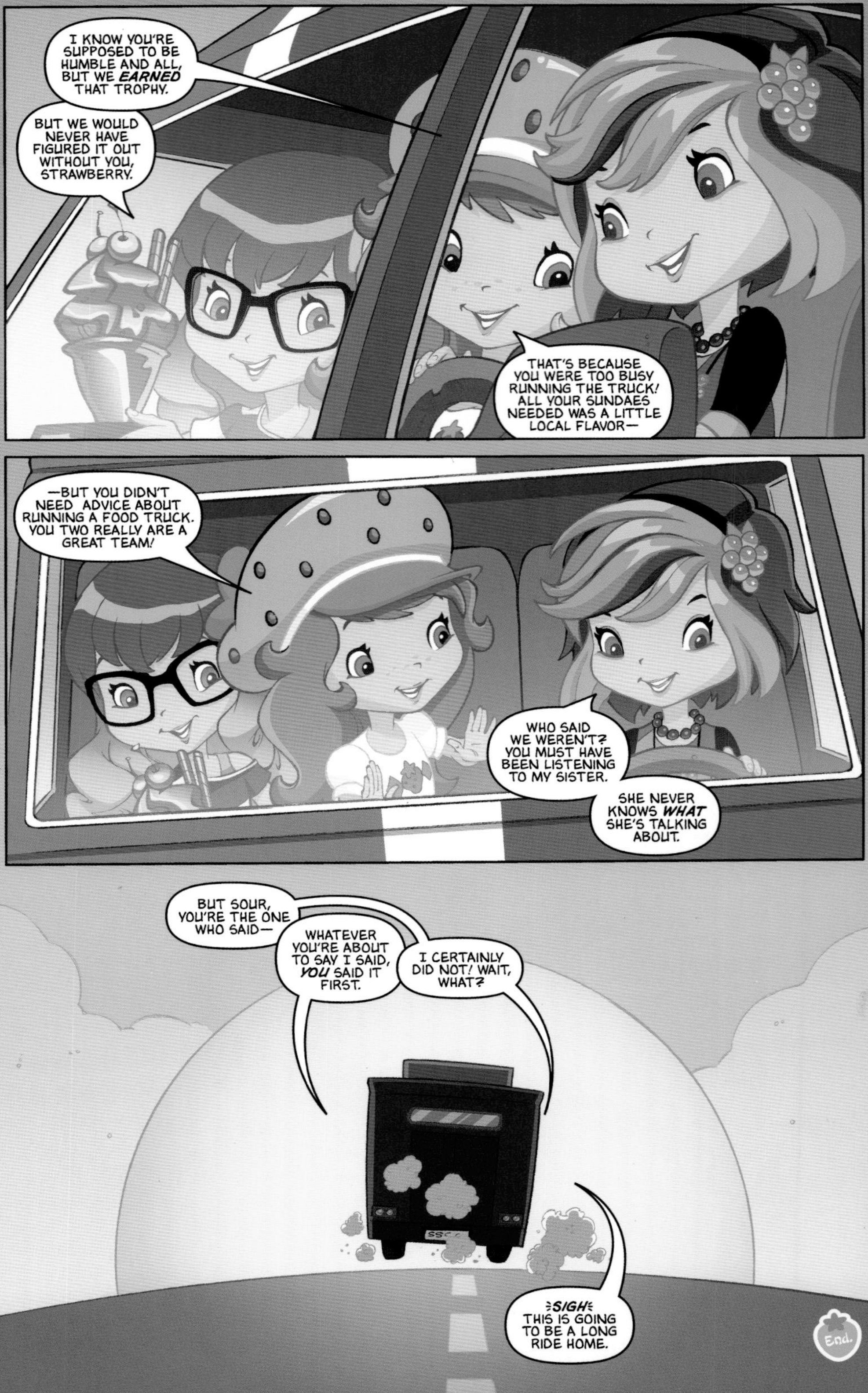
I KNOW YOU'RE SUPPOSED TO BE HUMBLE AND ALL, BUT WE ***EARNED*** THAT TROPHY.
BUT WE WOULD NEVER HAVE FIGURED IT OUT WITHOUT YOU, STRAWBERRY.
THAT'S BECAUSE YOU WERE TOO BUSY RUNNING THE TRUCK! ALL YOUR SUNDAES NEEDED WAS A LITTLE LOCAL FLAVOR—
—BUT YOU DIDN'T NEED ADVICE ABOUT RUNNING A FOOD TRUCK. YOU TWO REALLY ARE A GREAT TEAM!
WHO SAID WE WEREN'T? YOU MUST HAVE BEEN LISTENING TO MY SISTER.
SHE NEVER KNOWS ***WHAT*** SHE'S TALKING ABOUT.
BUT SOUR, YOU'RE THE ONE WHO SAID—
WHATEVER YOU'RE ABOUT TO SAY I SAID, ***YOU*** SAID IT FIRST.
I CERTAINLY DID NOT! WAIT, WHAT?
SIGH THIS IS GOING TO BE A LONG RIDE HOME.
End.

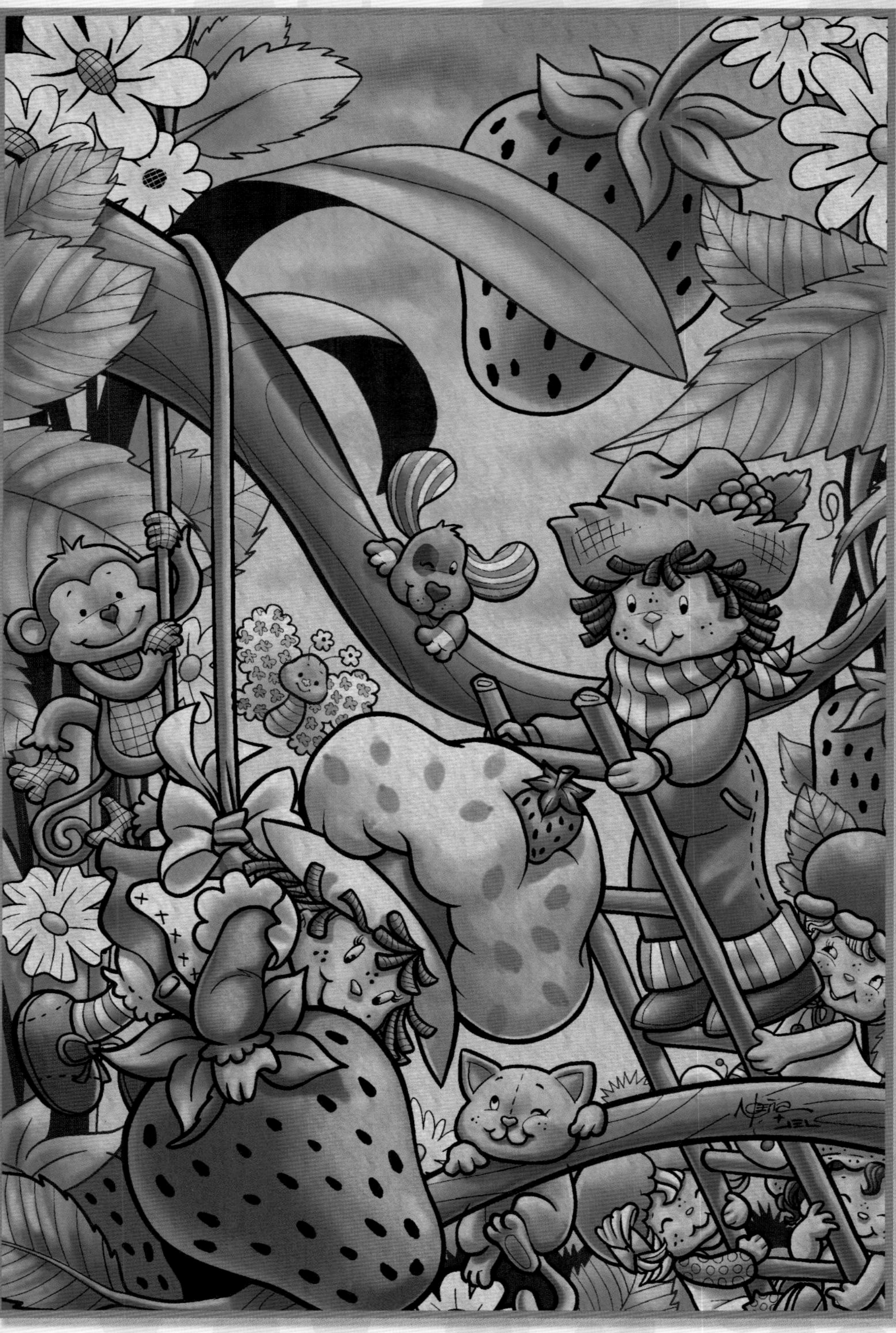

COVER ART BY Nico Peña

COVER COLORS BY Jordi Escuin

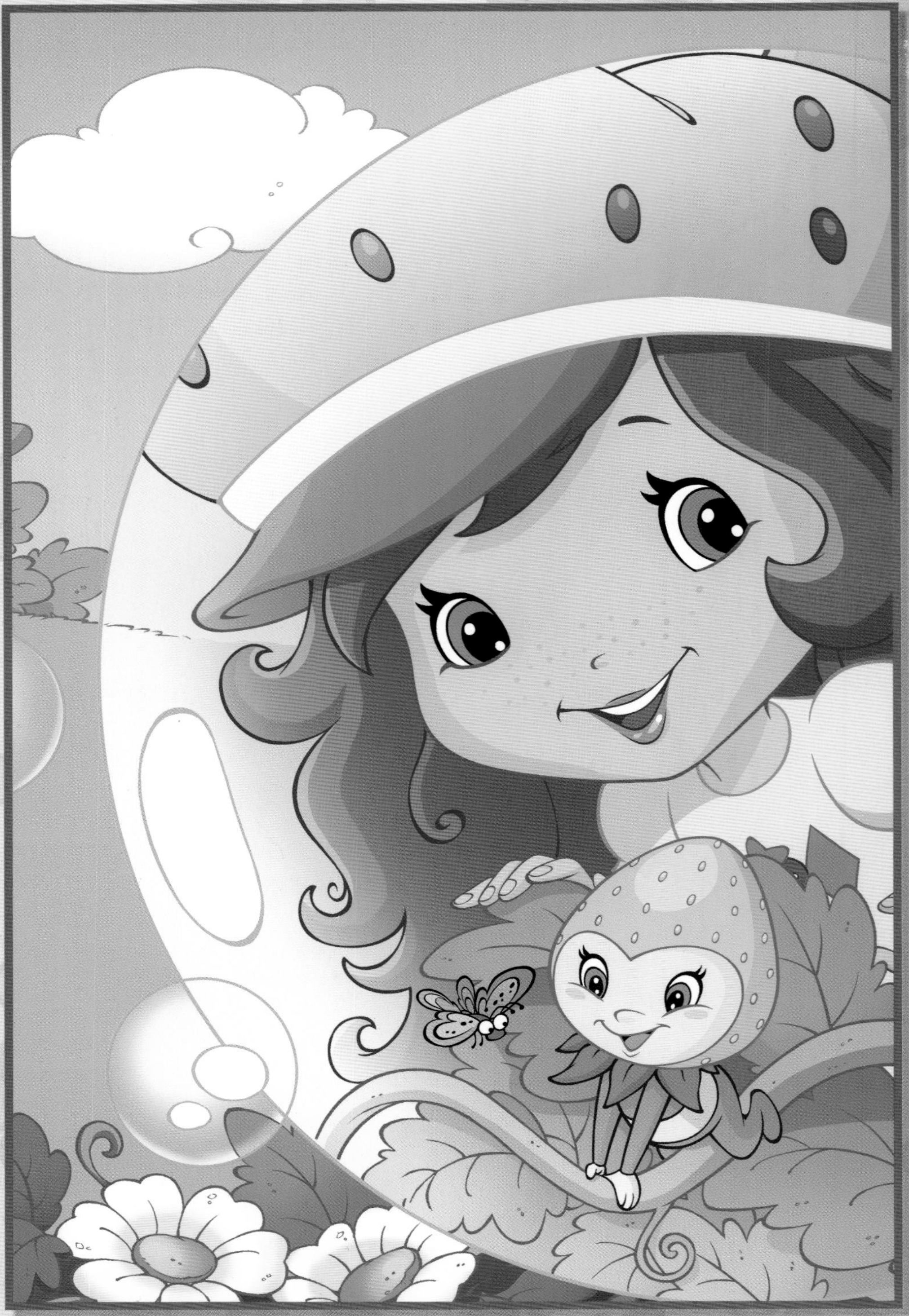

COVER ART BY Tina Franscisco

COVER COLORS BY Mae Hao

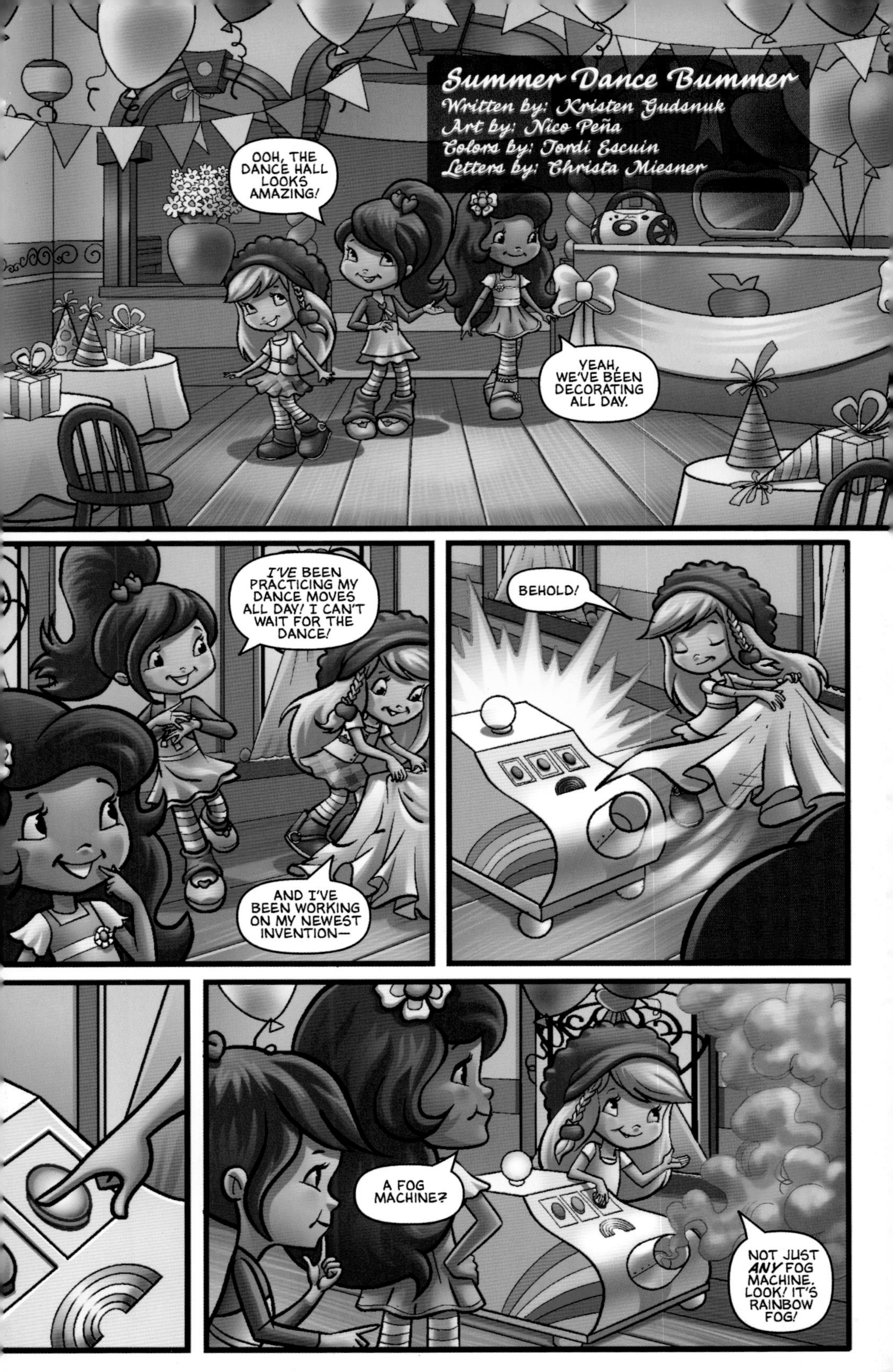
Summer Dance Bummer
Written by: Kristen Gudsnuk
Art by: Nico Peña
Colors by: Jordi Escuin
Letters by: Christa Miesner
OOH, THE DANCE HALL LOOKS AMAZING!
YEAH, WE'VE BEEN DECORATING ALL DAY.
I'VE BEEN PRACTICING MY DANCE MOVES ALL DAY! I CAN'T WAIT FOR THE DANCE!
AND I'VE BEEN WORKING ON MY NEWEST INVENTION—
BEHOLD!
A FOG MACHINE?
NOT JUST ANY FOG MACHINE. LOOK! IT'S RAINBOW FOG!

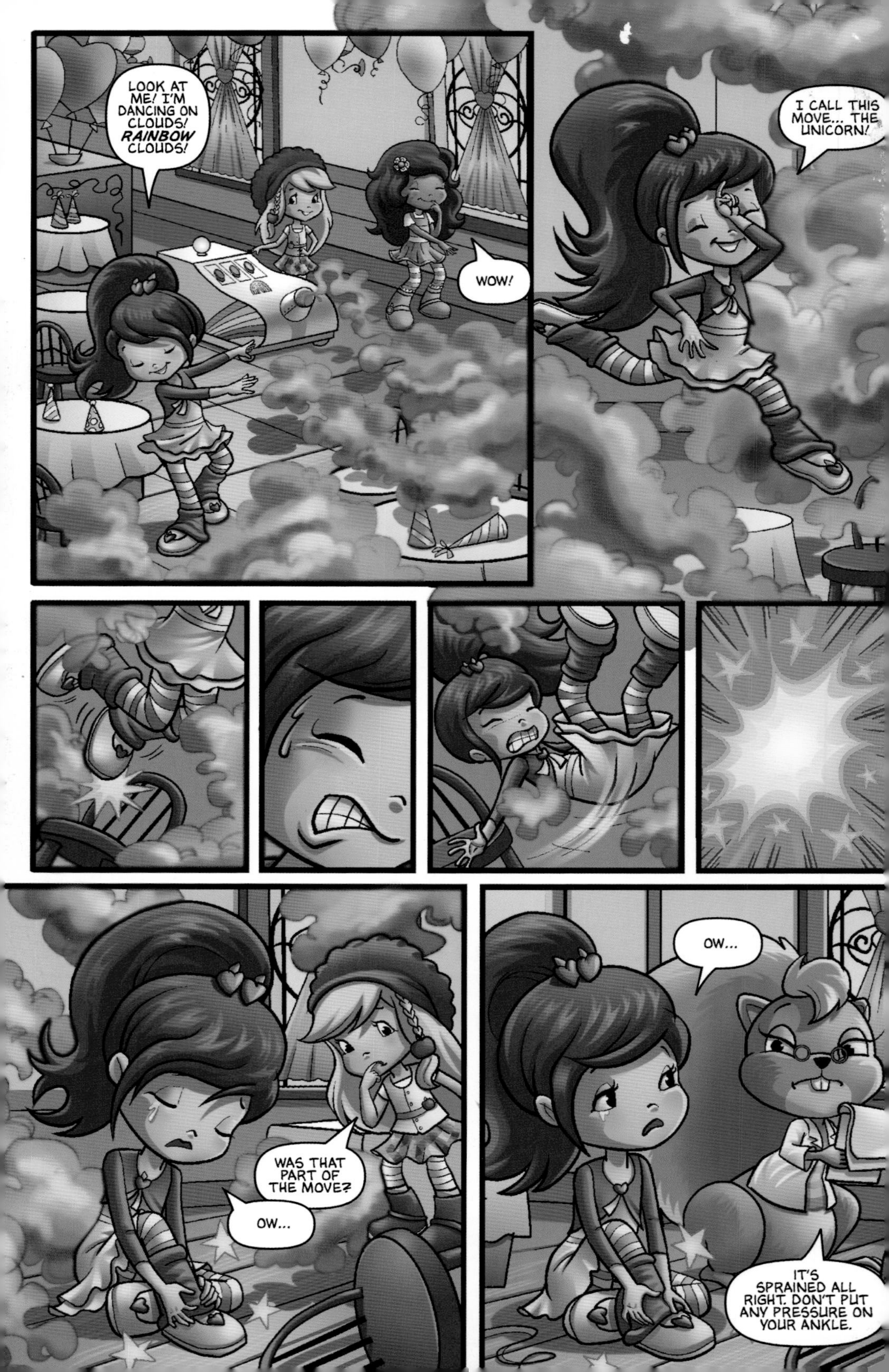

LOOK AT ME! I'M DANCING ON CLOUDS! ***RAINBOW*** CLOUDS!
WOW!
I CALL THIS MOVE... THE UNICORN!
WAS THAT PART OF THE MOVE?
OW...
OW...
IT'S SPRAINED ALL RIGHT. DON'T PUT ANY PRESSURE ON YOUR ANKLE.

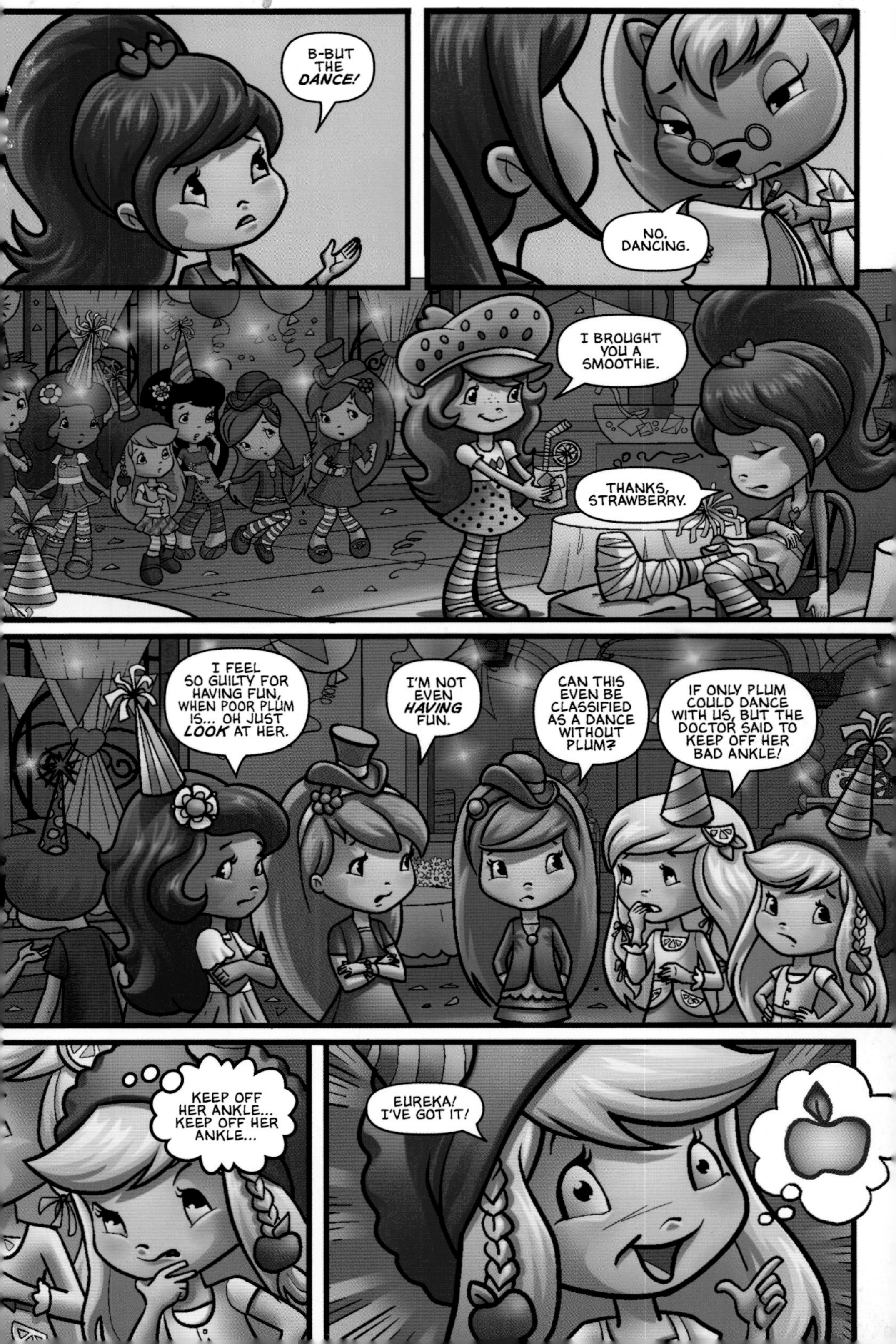
B-BUT THE DANCE!
NO. DANCING.
I BROUGHT YOU A SMOOTHIE.
THANKS, STRAWBERRY.
I FEEL SO GUILTY FOR HAVING FUN, WHEN POOR PLUM IS... OH JUST LOOK AT HER.
I'M NOT EVEN HAVING FUN.
CAN THIS EVEN BE CLASSIFIED AS A DANCE WITHOUT PLUM?
IF ONLY PLUM COULD DANCE WITH US, BUT THE DOCTOR SAID TO KEEP OFF HER BAD ANKLE!
KEEP OFF HER ANKLE... KEEP OFF HER ANKLE...
EUREKA! I'VE GOT IT!

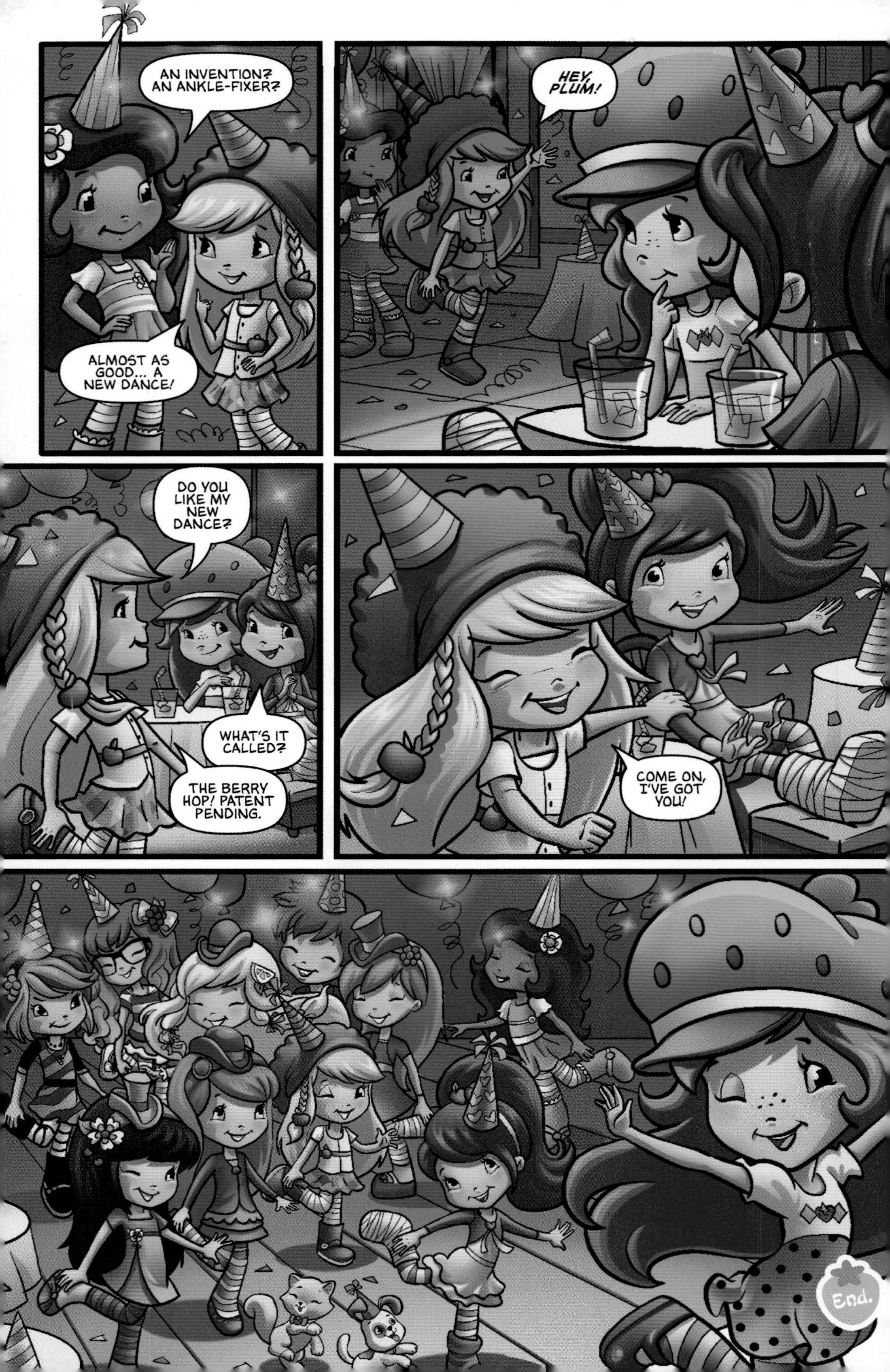
AN INVENTION? AN ANKLE-FIXER?
ALMOST AS GOOD... A NEW DANCE!
HEY, PLUM!
DO YOU LIKE MY NEW DANCE?
WHAT'S IT CALLED?
THE BERRY HOP! PATENT PENDING.
COME ON, I'VE GOT YOU!
End.

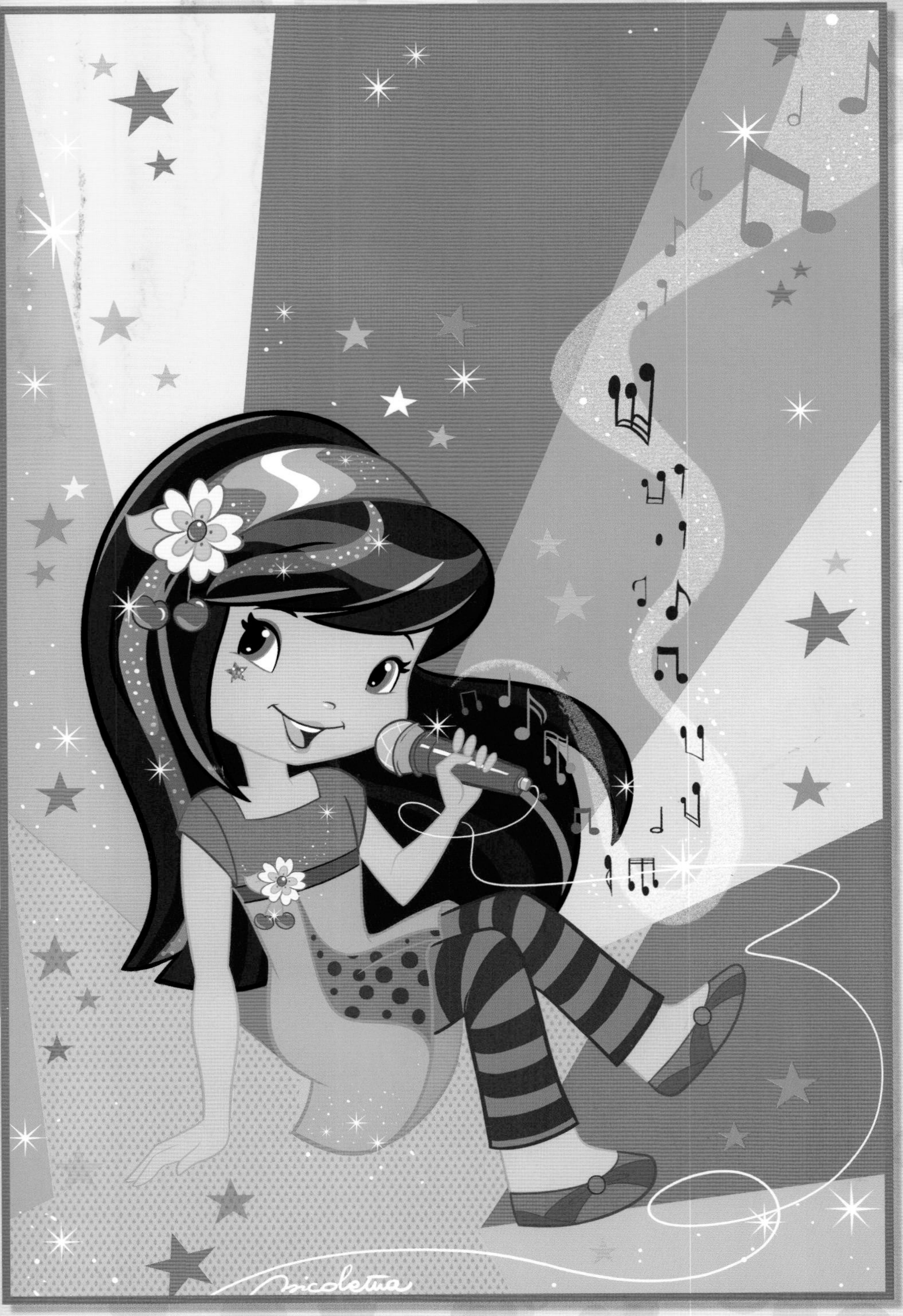
nicoletta

COVER ART BY Nicoletta Baldari

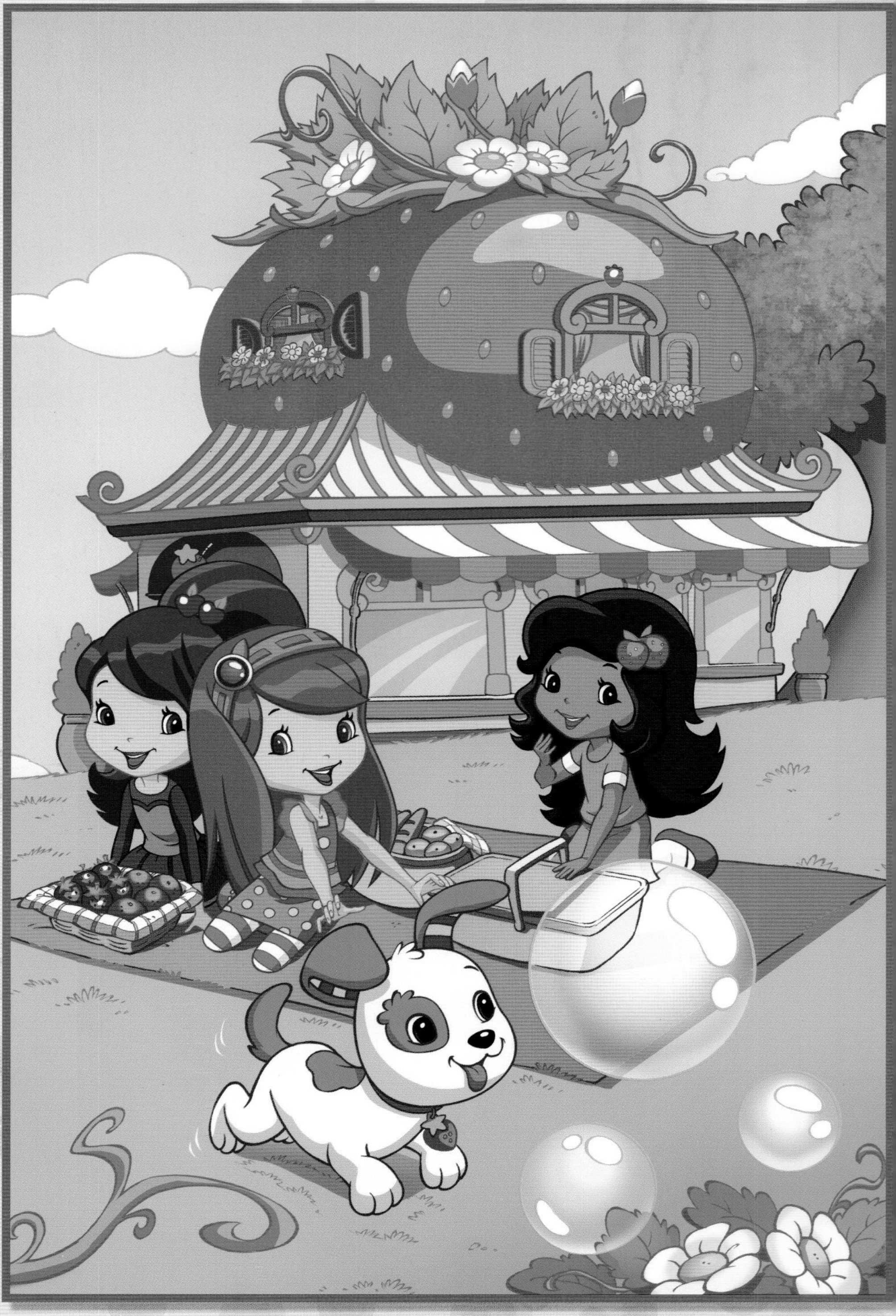

COVER ART BY Tina Franscisco

COVER COLORS BY Mae Hao

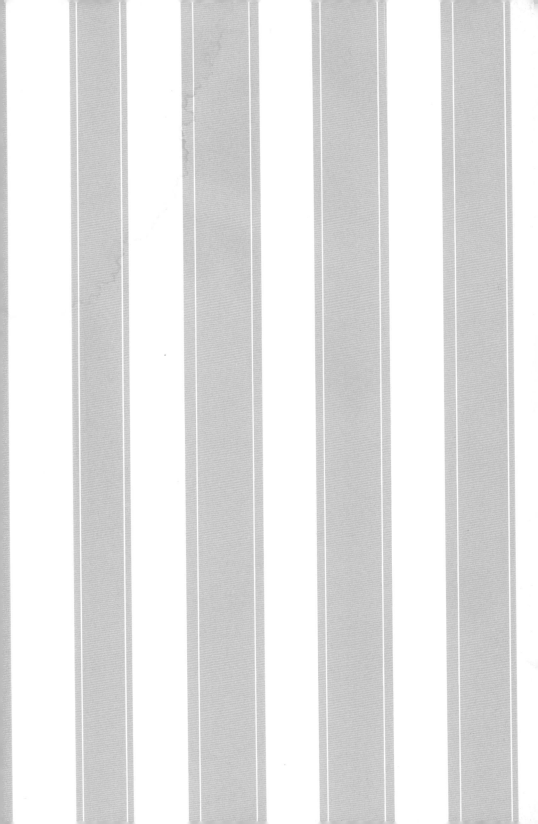